Dedication

This book is dedicated to anyone who has had to fight to protect the love that they had, and to the inspirational work of Alecia Beth Moore.

Project Magenta

Mike Gagnon

Published by Mike Gagnon, 2024.

This is a work of fiction. Similarities to real people, places, or events are entirely coincidental.

PROJECT MAGENTA

First edition. June 20, 2024.

ISBN: 978-1988369587

Written by Mike Gagnon.

Foreword

Ever had a song that feels like it speaks directly to your soul? For me, one of those is "Who Knew?" by P!NK. It's been playing in the background of my head for nearly two decades, weaving its way into my thoughts and inspiring this story that's been brewing in my mind all this time.

So, what's this story about? Well, it's a journey through life's ups and downs, loosely inspired by the emotions and themes in the song. It's about love found and lost, about taking risks and facing the consequences, about the unexpected twists and turns that shape our lives.

As you dive into these pages, I hope you'll feel the same connection to the emotions of the song that I do. Maybe you'll see echoes of your own experiences, or perhaps you'll discover something new about yourself. Either way, I'm excited for you to join me on this adventure fueled by the timeless magic of pop music. Let's see where the music takes us.

- Mike Gagnon, Feb. 2024

Chapter 1

Alecia navigated the bustling streets of Los Angeles on a crisp February morning. It was unremarkable in its simplicity, like many other mornings that she'd experienced, thanks to the perfect life that society afforded her in 2189. The megacity had grown beyond anything that her great-grandparents could have imagined, covering more than half the state of California. The city's size was due in large part to the economic growth and advancements of the last 100 years. The city's skyline towered over Alecia's short, naturally blonde but pink-dyed hair with its metal, glass, and concrete spires reaching for the sky. Every apartment building had at least one community greenhouse unit. Tenants found it much easier to pay rent when there was no danger of going hungry. Tall greenhouse skyscrapers, called Produce Towers, made sure that supermarkets always had a supply of fresh, locally grown produce. Impossibly suspended roads and bridges filled the airspace above and between the gray and glass buildings, while a variety of sky-bound vehicles zipped by; flying cars, cargo trucks, hover bikes, and something that Alecia thought looked like a cross between a helicopter and a praying mantis. All manner of flying vehicles flitted from building to building, other citizens rushing to work to start their day. Alecia had always believed she was born at the best time in history, and this cityscape reaffirmed her belief.

As she strolled towards a massive rectangular building, windowless with uninviting concrete walls, the Project Magenta Compound, Alecia's vibrant magenta spiked bangs caught the attention of a passerby. Another citizen walking about their business, shirtless with a leather harness, pants, face covwering mask complete with gas mask and combat boots. He was likely stumbling home from a late night at a local fetish club. The leather-clad stranger leered at Alecia, looking up and down, making sure that the nodding of his pale bald head conveyed an appreciation for how Alecia's burgundy leggings and gray hoodie worn over her pale pink t-shirt complemented her athletic, hourglass frame. It was clear that she was a woman who took pride in her appearance. In his appreciation of Alecia's passing body, the stranger failed to notice a small cluster of garbage sitting right next to one of the automated trash receptacles that lined the pedestrian walkway. The stranger's foot landed mid-pile and slid. Glancing over her shoulder, it appeared that her admirer had stepped in a large bag of dog shit. Without losing momentum, Alecia turned her head away, back toward the waiting security gate of Project Magenta, chuckling. The leather-clad stranger cursed his luck loudly to no one in particular, looking for something to scrape his boots clean with.

It was days like this that justified Alecia's vibrant exterior and made her feel like all of her past struggles in life had been worth it, for lack of a more nuanced term. Though she loved her life, her youth had not been easy, her subconscious memories carried a heavy burden. Every once in a while, she thought back to her childhood, to the day she was diagnosed with "An undefined Mild Cognitive Impairment" by Dr. Patrick. All that really meant was that Alecia sometimes lost entire days from her memory as if she had blacked out, and nobody seemed to be able to figure out why. She recalled when she had just turned twelve, sitting on a hospital bed in one of those embarrassing and drafty hospital gowns. Those gowns were just one small part of the reason that she hated hospitals. The time she'd spent in those places and those gowns had stolen a lot of her childhood. She remembered how the doctor emphatically explained to her how she was still "a normal person and it did not need to impact her life drastically". "Easy for him to say!" she had thought, though she knew that Dr. Patrick was doing his best to reassure a young patient. Doctor Patrick had a patient demeanour and kind smile below the coke-bottle glasses that amplified the size of his hazel eyes. When she thought of the dark features that he'd inherited from his Haitian mother, she held no bitterness and knew that he had genuinely cared about her well-being, as well as his other patients. The memory of her father, Brian, holding her hand tightly during that diagnosis still lingered in her mind. A big, strong, Hispanic tower of a man, Brian Hernandez's 6'6" frame could make many wanna-be tough guys cower, but to Alecia, he was just a big teddy bear. Lung cancer had taken him in 2182, shortly after she'd completed her University education, but Alecia chose to cling to the happy memories she had of him and not what cancer had done to him in his later years. Working on cars in the semi-detached garage of her family's suburban California home, talking about life, and listening to her mom's old music files were some of her favourite memories. That, and her father's steady, hand-holding support during all of those hospital visits, while some of the most highly trained doctors in the world tried to figure out why she missed chunks of her memory. Those blank spells, the lost moments in time, had taken on a haunting quality, ever since his loss.

The Compound loomed ahead, its imposing concrete structure a stark contrast to the surrounding urban landscape. Alecia knew that within those dark corridors and metallic walls lay the secrets of the Time Well, a device that allowed time travel and was closely guarded by the military. She flashed her face to the security panel, framed on either side by two of the armed military police that comprised the security force for the compound. The secrets of time travel and access to it had become the most heavily guarded asset within the United Socialist Democracies of North America, USDNA for short, since the government had disclosed the project's existence in 2178. The Time Well was a major reason why the young country, formed in 2099 by the merger of the United States, Canada, and Mexico, maintained a role as one of the most powerful and prosperous nations on Earth.

Inside the Compound, Alecia's coworkers were already busy at work. She quickly padded toward the co-ed civilian employee locker room and stripped. From her locker, she grabbed a gray coverall and pulled it up over her body. The high-tech bodysuit covered her from neck to toe, the thick durable fabric hiding all sorts of high-tech sensors that would heat or cool the wearer as required, based on the environment that they were working in. Thin pink LED strips down the legs and under the arms glowed as the suit adjusted to Alecia's body temperature. The glowing strips activated every time the suit performed a function, such as temperature adjustments or self-cleaning, keeping the wearer aware that its hidden microcomputers were performing functions properly. Alecia's favourite feature was the ample thigh pockets, which made it easy for her to always have a wrench, ratchet, screwdriver, knife, wire stripper, and other tools quickly at hand. From the top shelf of the locker, she grabbed her safety glasses, a wide band of dark elastic with large round copper frames and dark lenses, a vintage item that her father had found at an estate auction and gifted to her for their garage projects. Alecia thought the goggles somewhat resembled an old-timey aviator's helmet, but the antiquity of the item only made her love and cherish the gift even more. Alecia pulled her safety glasses on and exited the locker room into the massive, rusty metal walls of the Time Well's engine room. She exchanged greetings with the familiar faces of co-workers, as they rushed to find tools, move a welding cart, or weave between the metal racks of tools, machinery parts, metal pipes, and sheeting that lined the exterior of the massive workshop. The farthest wall of the engine room, opposite the locker room entrance, was the home of a metal platform topped with a massive heavy equipment crane that was mounted to the ceiling on rails, which allowed it to move large objects in the room from side to side. The metal plate centred at the base of the crane was framed on either side by 2 massive and identical engines. The stainless steel outer casings glinted like polished chrome, rising in a rounded arc from the floor to about 30 feet high at the center of its arch. The housing had slits cut into the metal to allow heat to escape and provide visuals to some of the working parts, should a mechanic need to take a look while diagnosing a problem. Small control panels and component housings seemed to grow out of the sides of the metal casing at the person level, allowing mechanics to run diagnostics, exchange parts, or access the inner workings as needed. Alecia grinned as she nonchalantly padded over to a workbench, leaning on it and addressing a co-worker who was standing on a large stool while hunched over the workbench, cursing at some rusted metal part that he couldn't get to separate from another rusted metal part. "Hey Benny, what do we get the privilege of fixing today?" Benny Hurley was an Australian Aboriginal with a penchant for fixing things, and as made evident by his step stool and small stature, he also happened to be a little person. Benny had a no-nonsense attitude and always had a witty remark ready. Benny wore a set of coveralls that matched Alecia's, however, his uniform included a full helmet with a tinted face visor. Having grown up in a place where people are killed by falling coconuts, Benny was hyper-aware of head protection, possibly to an obsessive degree. His open visor allowed him a better look at his task, which apparently helped little, as there was no change in the free-flowing complaints that he issued.

"We have to replace these bloody couplers for the coolant lines again!" Benny exclaimed in exasperation. "It's just, you know, *TIME TRAVEL!*" he continued, to no one. "Heaven forbid they get us some decent couplers that the bloody coolant doesn't corrode away every other week! No problem, it's not as if it's for something important, we'll just keep changing these bloody rubbish iron couplers every couple of weeks!"

Alecia chuckled and reached for her ratchet as Benny released a forlorn sigh of impotent anger. She then held her first aloft, Benny grinned and did the same in response, bumping fists to be followed with each of them opening their hand and pulling it back while making imaginary explosion noises. The pair padded over to the time lab, Alecia excitedly holding her ratchet aloft in the air with mock victory and Benny carrying a large netted bag full of iron couplers over his shoulder. The experienced duo would make short work of this coupler exchange.

The time lab was a large open room with curved metallic walls. A smattering of workstations, complete with scientists in lab coats. High-end scientific computers and equipment were spread out in the open areas around the massive chamber. In the center of the time lab was the Time Well, the heart of Project Magenta. The Time Well consisted of a platform and control panel mounted on a metal grating, which made it look as if it was hovering in the air. An additional wall of metal chain link rose from behind the control panel, allowing all of the necessary screens and control equipment to be mounted securely above the main controls. Below the platform was a circular opening about 20 feet wide over a 20-foot-deep pit, complete with metal access ladders for personnel to climb up and down on.

Benny climbed down to the bottom of the pit with his bag of couplers, followed by Alecia, who began using her ratchet to remove a row of curved metal panels from the wall, running next to the access ladder. Alecia would remove the panels, then Benny would curse as he climbed the ladder, pulling coolant hoses out and replacing couplers before returning the hoses in place, with Alecia following him and the replacing wall panels to their original position, one at a time, all the way back up.

After securing the final metal panel next to the ladder, Alecia crawled out of the pit and was happy to see the lab coat-clad Dr. Gail Agu approaching her. Dr. Agu, a thin woman of 72 years, whose dark complexion revealed her Ethiopian descent, supervised the Time Force assignments. Gail was known for her analytical mind at work and as a lover of fine wine and ballroom dancing to her friends. Despite their age difference, Alecia had formed a strong bond with Gail over the years. Gail approached with a knowing grin and a sideways look through the delicate, thin-framed spectacles that perched atop her pointed features to Alecia. It was the kind of look usually exchanged between friends or co-workers who don't have to say anything to know what they are thinking. They both looked towards Benny, who was walking away and still grumbling about iron couplers. They looked back at each other and laughed as Dr. Gail brushed a silver-streaked wisp of white curls, which had been black in her youth, behind her ear, in an attempt to convince it to rejoin the rest of its family in the tight bun that she normally wore at work. "Thank you so much, guys." Dr. Agu commented to Alecia, loud enough that she hoped Benny would hear too. "We couldn't run this place without you." "You know it!" Alecia agreed with a smile as she began to pad away, trying to catch up with Benny.

The pair of mechanics hesitated in their path back to the engine room. They encountered two darkly clad men entering the lab from an opening in the shiny, curved walls that led to the military locker room, reserved for Time Force officers. Both men were clad in the same black body stocking, adorned with dark gray padding on the chest, spine, shoulders, thighs, shins, knees, elbows, forearms, and groin, all standard-issue and necessary protection for the falls that the officers were expected to take in the Time Well. Alecia always wondered why they never bothered to wear helmets.

As Benny passed the pair he grinned, turned, and shouted into the cacophonous room. "Here come the hot shots!" He continued without losing a step, chuckling as good-natured laughs and sporadic clapping broke out among the scientists at their workstations.

The first man was Officer Dale Yoshawa, a fourth-generation Japanese American, with a short dark military buzz cut that somehow only served to compliment his complexion, brown eyes, and athletic build. "Hey there beautiful." Officer Yoshawa said to Alecia with a playful wink as he passed. Alecia felt a flutter in her chest and a rush of blood to her face. Truth be told, when Dale Yoshawa looked at her like that, it sent an involuntary shiver of anticipation down her spine. She smiled back at Dale and responded good-naturedly, loud enough for bystanders to hear, "Save the charm for your official assignments, Officer Yoshawa." This elicited a few more disembodied chuckles from the science staff in the lab.

Officer Yoshawa was followed closely by his investigative partner, Officer Kevin Kilroy. Aside from being Time Officers and having black hair, Kilroy and Yoshawa had very little in common. They got along well, respecting each other as equals thanks to a friendship built on years of having each other's backs when working investigations away from the Time Lab. Where Yoshawa's hair was trimmed short, Kilroy had let his hair grow out, sweeping his locks into one voluminous wave that swooshed from his forehead to the back of his head, almost like a pompadour. The eastern European features twisted into a lecherous leer that oozed indecency as he passed Alecia. "Damn right, we're the hotshots!" Officer Kilroy proudly announced, arrogantly peacocking across the time lab toward his pre-jump briefing with Dr. Agu.

Where Officer Yoshawa made Alecia's heart flutter, Kilroy made her sick to her stomach. She tolerated his sleaziness and innuendo as much as she could, and only to keep from causing any potential conflicts with Dale over his partner.

Together, Alecia and Benny returned to work on the time engines, the massive machines responsible for generating the power needed for the Time Well. The pair had worked together at Project Magenta since Alecia first started as a trainee. Benny had several years under his belt already when Alecia had started, and where others were fooled by his gruff exterior and cranky temperament, Alecia saw the heart of gold hidden underneath. The pair had become fast friends and Alecia's natural skills and talents were quickly enhanced thanks to Benny taking her under his wing. This is how they developed their signature tag-team approach to the day-to-day maintenance of the machinery in the massive concrete compound. They had become a formidable team, complementing each other's skills effortlessly.

As the morning progressed, the team prepared for a significant time jump. Dr. Agu took charge of coordinating the operation, ensuring everything was in place, and debriefing the Time Officers on mission objectives. Alecia watched with a mix of anticipation and curiosity as Dale prepared for today's jump.

With a sense of ceremony, the Time Lab came to life. Dr. Agu strode onto the Time Well platform, tapping fingers quickly across the transparent control panel that nearly appeared to float above the bank of computers and bright buttons. Moments later, the circuitry that ran along the gaping circular opening of the Time Well generated a thin, rippling pink layer of temporal energy over the 20-foot-deep pit. At the bottom of that pit, motion-triggered airbags and heavy padding awaited the Time Officer's descent.

Dale stepped onto the platform, his gaze briefly locking with Alecia's, who had stolen a moment away from her engine work to sneak a peek, bashfully half-hidden by the entrance between the engine room and the lab. Another perk of having a tag-team approach was that she and Benny could handle working on jobs alone when necessary or if one of them just needed a breather. Alecia often snuck away to watch on the days that Dale was "dropping in" to the well. There was a connection between them, a silent understanding of the risks and responsibilities that came with their work.

"Are you ready?" Dr. Agu issued her standard pre-jump question. "Ready and willing," Dale responded excitedly. "Remember, as important as our mission is, today's objective is to simply verify the date and location of the subject, beyond that, it's just a regular day." the doctor confirmed. "Copy that." With a nod to Dr. Agu, Dale took a deep breath and let himself tip backward, arms raised as he plummeted into the Time Well, disappearing into the temporal energy below.

The lab fell into a momentary hush, the anticipation palpable. Then, with a loud thud, Dale reappeared at the bottom of the pit, cushioned by the airbags. He climbed the ladder, his mind filled with memories of an objective completed in the past.

Alecia released a breath that she hadn't realized she'd been holding until that moment. As Dale climbed out of the pit he shot a sideways glance at Alecia and smiled. Alecia smiled back, and then remembering her duties, turned back to the busy engine room, only slightly blushing.

As Officer Yoshawa and Dr. Agu went to debrief with the Time Directors and analyze the jump, Alecia couldn't help but feel a surge of pride and admiration for him, and the immense responsibility and trust put in someone tasked with jumping through time.

After a long day at the Compound, Alecia and Dale returned to their luxurious condo. "Nice to be home after a long day, eh *Mrs.* Yoshawa?" Dale asked, opening the door into their unit for his blushing bride. "Yes, it is, *Mr.* Yoshawa." Alecia said, putting the same emphasis on the word "Mister" that he had on "Misses". She put her arms around his neck and leaned forward to place a deep kiss on his lips.

As the pair entered their home, the space exuded a sense of minimalist comfort, a place where they could unwind after the rigours of their work. Alecia's mother's old music recordings played softly in the background as they moved through their nightly routine.

After checking for any messages that may have come in on the tele-corder during the day, Alecia and Dale made their way to the bathroom where they brushed their teeth and talked about their day. Following their ablutions, Alecia was no longer able to resist placing her hands on either side of Dale's face and planting a long, deep passionate kiss on his lips, outdoing the one she'd planted on him at the doorway by several degrees. They shared an intimate moment, staring into each other's eyes before Alecia backed away and wordlessly stripped nude, giving him a grin before sliding open the floor-to-ceiling glass wall and entering the spacious steam shower with overhead rainfall setting. Alecia's nude body was the perfect canvas to show off the intricate and detailed tattoo of a Japanese cherry blossom tree that ran up the full left side of her ribcage. Dale smiled and thought about how lucky he was before following suit by stripping, showing off his own full-back Japanese dragon tattoo, and entering the shower behind her. Steam clouds and trickles of warm water cascaded over them, cleansing away the stress of the day. Their bodies pressed close, and their connection was undeniable. As soon as the soap was rinsed out of the way, their hands and mouths began exploring each other's bodies, releasing all of the pent-up sexual tension and stress of the day.

Their lovemaking carried them, half-dried from their shower, into the bedroom. Their union was a passionate dance between two souls deeply in love. Their mutual passion for discovering each other's pleasure zones filled their condo with sighs and moans. Afterward, as they lay together in bed, sated and content, Alecia's curiosity got the best of her.

"Dale," she began, her voice soft, "what's it like to time jump?"

Dale turned to her, his eyes filled with a mixture of memories and emotions. "Well, it's kinda hard to explain," he started. "You have just the briefest split-second of being somewhere with no direction, filled with bright colours..."

"And then you wake up in the past, at the beginning of the day, in your own, younger body," Dale added after a brief pause. "And you have about 24 hours, give or take, to complete your mission. When you fall asleep, you drop back out of the Time Well, make a brief verbal report for the microphones, and then spend the rest of the shift debriefing with the Time Directors.

He described the sensation of time travel, the disorienting experience of inhabiting a younger body, and the rush of fulfilling an assigned objective. Alecia listened intently, fascinated by the intricacies of her husband's work.

After laying together in a post-coitus cuddle, Alecia looked at Dale and said "Want a coffee?" "I'd love one!" Dale replied. The pair rose and slipped on their underwear, they rarely felt the need to be completely clothed when at home. As Alecia fastened her bra and Dale slid a tight undershirt over his body, their ongoing conversation about time jumping and the debriefing process was interrupted when Dale's voice shuddered. He released a hard, loud, involuntary cough and collapsed, smashing with a hard "THUD" into the staircase that led up from their bedroom to the rest of the condo.

"Dale!" Alecia shouted in wide-eyed surprise, panic setting in when she realized that he was breathing, but could not be stirred back into consciousness.

Chapter 2

The sterile white walls of the hospital room enclosed Alecia and Dale Yoshawa as they sat on the edge of a clinical-looking bed. Dr. Celia Grant, a middle-aged physician with long messy brown hair, a slim build, large round glasses, and a pale complexion, gave a warm, but troubled expression. She stood before them, holding a transparent digital clipboard that displayed a series of moving charts and images that nobody outside of a trained physician would be able to make heads or tails of.

"Mr. and Mrs. Yoshawa," Dr. Grant began, her voice gentle but tinged with sorrow, "I've reviewed all the test results three times and consulted with several of my colleagues. I'm afraid I have news that is going to be difficult to hear."

Alecia's heart pounded in her chest as she exchanged a worried glance with Dale. She gripped his hand tightly.

"Your husband," Dr. Grant continued, "has an advanced case of Cerebral Lymphoma. It's a very rare form of brain cancer...I...I'm sorry to say it's already spread too far to consider conventional treatment. I'm so sorry."

From the doctor trying to restrain her own emotions while delivering the news, Dale and Alecia quickly realized that this may have been the worst news that they could have gotten.

Dale swallowed hard, his face paling. Alecia felt her throat tighten as tears welled up in her eyes. She turned to the doctor, desperation in her voice. "Isn't there anything you can do, Doctor? Anything at all?"

Dr. Grant sighed, her expression sympathetic. "I wish there were, Mrs. Yoshawa, but given the stage of the disease, it's beyond our current capabilities to treat effectively. We can provide palliative care to make him as comfortable as possible. With regular treatment and care, we can extend life expectancy by 1 to 2 years. Without treatment, Dale may only have a few months. Again, I'm so, so sorry to be giving you this news."

Through his shock, Dale feebly managed to rasp out a question. "What could have caused it?"

"We still don't know all of the causes for this type of cancer." Dr. Grant explained. "There's been a lot of speculation about possible radiation exposure from your job with time travel, but there's never been any clinical proof of such claims. At the end of the day, the technology is just too new for us to know if there is any connection."

Alecia felt a wave of despair wash over her. She couldn't bear the thought of losing Dale, her love, her rock. A glimmer of hope flashed in her mind, the kind of idea that is borne of extreme desperation.

"What about the Time Well?" Alecia blurted out. "Can't we use it to go back and prevent this from happening?"

Dr. Grant's eyes widened in shock, and she took a step back. "Mrs. Yoshawa, you can't be serious," she stammered. "Using the Time Well for personal reasons, especially to change a medical diagnosis, is illegal. It goes against everything the Time Force stands for. If I thought you were serious, I'd have to report it."

Alecia's frustration and anger boiled over. She jumped to her feet, her face contorted with emotion. "You people and your rules! You have the technology to change the past, to save lives, but that's not allowed. This man puts his ass on the line every day to make the world better for you and everyone else, but when he needs that same kind of help, you just WON'T do anything!"

Dale reached out and placed a calming hand on Alecia's shoulder. "Leesh, please," he implored softly, "I know you're hurting, I can't even process my own feelings yet, but you know how serious the responsibility of changing the past is. We can't break the law."

Alecia's anger slowly ebbed, replaced by a profound sense of resentment and action. She turned to Dr. Grant, tears streaming down her face. "I'm sorry, Doctor, but none of this is acceptable. We'll be getting a second opinion, hell a third opinion, and if the diagnosis *is* correct, come hell or high water, I'm going to find someone who can help him." Alecia strode purposely toward the exit, propelled by her anger. "Grab your coat, Dale, we're getting out of here!"

Dale, jacket in hand, gave Dr. Grant a sombre look as he passed. "I'm sorry Doc," he said. Dr. Grant placed a comforting hand on Dale's shoulder. "No, I'm sorry, Mr. Yoshawa." "Thank you," Dale said softly, then continued toward the exit, following Alecia.

As Alecia stormed over to their parked hovercar, her resolve solidified. She couldn't give up on Dale. She would do whatever it took to save him, and she didn't give a rat's ass about what the laws were if something could save him and keep him with her. "It's crazy to tell someone they're going to die without confirming it with another opinion first." She half shouted as Dale trailed behind, a mix of emotions and thoughts that he couldn't verbalize yet.

Over the next few weeks, Alecia and Dale sought other opinions from various doctors. Dr. Fred Glumpf and Dr. James Botell each independently confirmed the same thing that Dale and Alecia already knew. Each time, they received the same grim prognosis: Dale's condition was terminal, and there was no hope for a cure.

Desperation led them to their last hope within Project Magenta itself—Dr. Gail Agu. Gail had been a practicing physician before time travel had been disclosed. She was one of many who were swept up in the new branch of science that was suddenly available. Gail had always enjoyed helping patients with medical ailments, but time travel lit a fire of passion for exploration in her mind that propelled her to work every day in a way that medicine never had. Gail was able to coax the nurse practitioners to let her use some of the high-tech medical equipment that was located in Project Magenta's medical bay while they were on a lunch break. She'd have to make a point of bringing the Med Staff a round of coffees the next morning. With access to advanced medical equipment and technology, Dr. Agu performed exhaustive tests on

Dale. Small pointed scanners that looked like pink highlighters were connected to long, curved metal arms that rose up, connected to tracks on the ceiling that allowed a computer to move and manipulate the location of the scanner. Several of these "pink highlighters" whirled quickly around Dale's ever-thinning body, draped in the classic hospital gown that Alecia had such a distaste for. The sensors continued to whirl and spin, occasionally making a "beep" noise, followed by a brief pinpoint of light emitted from the sensor. The sensors fed information to a transparent screen mounted on the end of the hospital bed on which Dale lay, being viewed by Dr. Agu. Alecia held her breath, praying for a miracle.

After a second round of complete scans, Dr. Agu removed her gloves and sighed, her expression grave. She met Alecia's eyes and gently shook her head.

"I'm so sorry, Alecia," she said softly. "There's nothing more we can do. His condition is beyond treatment."

Alecia's shoulders slumped, and she felt the weight of the world on her. All their efforts, all their hopes, had led to this same devastating conclusion. Dale was wasting away before her eyes, and there was nothing she could do to stop it.

Dale had been taken off of active duty the day that he had been diagnosed, leaving Officer Kilroy to handle the caseload on his own until a new trainee could be assigned to help him. Since Dale was no longer active, Dr. Agu and Alecia had to arrange a temporary security pass to let Dale into the building as a visitor. The application had taken weeks to process and then they had to choose a day that Alecia was not working to pull off their impromptu exam. As required by security protocols in the compound, Dr. Agu escorted Alecia and Dale to the security entrance to leave, as the pair clung to each other, their love and despair intertwined. The world outside seemed to blur for them as they faced an uncertain future together, determined to make every moment count.

Chapter 3

The mood in Alecia and Dale Yoshawa's condo was one of camaraderie and celebration. Alecia had decided to throw a party. Thanks to an extensive regimen of medical treatments, Dale had survived a year since his diagnosis. Alecia was hoping that a night of fun with friends would lift Dale's spirits, take his mind off of his looming mortality, and surround him with friends who would encourage him to keep fighting. The living room was filled with laughter and chatter as attendees enjoyed food and drinks, sharing stories and memories.

Among the guests were familiar faces from Project Magenta. Alecia knew she looked cute in her black bodice and knee-length skirt, with matching combat boots. Shiny metal spikes and chains accented the outfit. She looked the epitome of punk rocker chic. Dale wore the outfit that had become a trademark since his health took a turn, comfortable gray sweatpants and matching hoodie, his new uniform as a sick person. Kevin Kilroy was still in his Military Police uniform, though not straight from work. Benny had traded his helmet and coveralls for a very smart Brown vest and slacks combo over a nice white dress shirt. It was early in the evening, but Benny was already drunk and topless, dancing on the coffee table and swinging his once crisply pressed shirt over his head. Dr. Gail Agu was the picture of elegant sophistication. A short-sleeved black pantsuit with a plunging neckline showed just enough skin to still be tasteful. Dr. Agu was proud of the figure she'd maintained into her seventies, a few wrinkles were a sign of experience and pride, not a reason not to show some skin. Her hair was taken out of the bun she reserved for the workplace and had been styled into a pair of Odango buns on the back of either side of her head. Dr. Agu's delicate thin-rimmed, black-framed glasses had been traded for gold, matching her sparkling bracelet and necklace. Reina Yoshawa, Dale's mother, watched mostly from a chair in the living room. Aside from Gail, everyone in the room was much younger, which made sense, they were her son's friends, and she was just there to comfort and support him as much as she could when needed. She wore a crisply tailored navy blue power suit, one of a selection that she wore to court as a family law attorney. Reina sat nervously, sipping a soda and making polite chit-chat with the other guests when they approached her. Jane Jones-Miller and Bill Jones-Miller rounded out the guest list. Bill was a fellow Time Officer and co-worker of Dale and Kevin's. Unlike Kilroy, Bill had managed to change out of his work uniform and into a beige button-down shirt with matching khakis, his long brown hair swept back and to the side. Jane Jones-Miller had bonded with Alecia over the fact that they were both military wives. Beyond that one item, Jane and Alecia didn't really have that much in common. Where Alecia's hair was short and bright, Jane's was long and dark. Where Alecia was a tan color, thanks to her mixed heritage, Jane was pale, except for some sunburn, thanks to the days she spent working in one of the city's many fresh produce towers. She was a very pleasant and polite person with simple needs and a matching wardrobe, a peasant-style lace camisole and jeans. Several other random friends and co-workers also popped in and out throughout the course of the evening, adding to the lively atmosphere.

Alecia moved gracefully through the crowd, her radiant smile and vibrant energy infecting everyone around her. She was determined to make this a night to remember, not just for Dale but for all their friends who had come to support them.

As the evening wore on, Alecia and Dr. Gail Agu found themselves in the kitchen, away from the hubbub of the party. Alecia's smile faded as she looked into Gail's eyes, her concern etched across her face. Secretly, this upcoming conversation was another reason that she had held this party. Going the way that she wanted it to was crucial to an idea she'd been brewing since Dale's diagnosis.

"Gail," Alecia began quietly, "I need your help."

Gail raised an eyebrow, her expression curious. "What do you need, Alecia?"

Alecia hesitated for a moment, her voice barely above a whisper. "I need you to help us use the Time Well to save Dale."

Gail's eyes widened in shock, and she took a step back. "Alecia, you know I can't do that. It's not only illegal, but it's also morally wrong. We can't use time travel for personal gain or to alter the past for our own benefit."

Alecia's frustration flared, and she clenched her fists. "Morally wrong? Gail, you can save his life! How can you stand by and do nothing?"

Gail sighed, her gaze filled with empathy. "Alecia, I understand your desperation, but there are consequences to altering the past. It could have unintended ripple effects, and we can't predict the outcome. Besides, it's against everything we stand for at Project Magenta."

Alecia felt her heartache, torn between her love for Dale and her respect for Gail... and for the principles of time travel. "Oh, it's against the rules, so you just let him die?" Alecia glared intensely. "That's what our friendship is worth to you?" Gail, taken aback momentarily with a pang of guilt and pain, tempered with understanding, took a breath and responded firmly. "It's not worth compromising my principles and endangering others, no."

Now it was Alecia's turn to look momentarily hurt, no matter how misguided, before mentally regrouping, "Gee, thanks for coming to our party Gail. Help yourself to the appetizers, booze is in the cupboard." Alecia's words did not match the glare that she was directing at Gail. With a cold, determined look, she turned away from her friend and rejoined the party, leaving the doctor too flabbergasted to respond. Gail slowly and awkwardly walked back out to the living room, her mind a painful mix of guilt, sympathy, and self-doubt.

Shortly after Alecia's return from the kitchen, Dale excused himself and headed to the washroom. He felt a sense of unease wash over him.

He could feel his body growing weaker by the day. He turned to Alecia, "I'm just gonna go powder my nose for a minute." "You okay?" Alecia's face was a picture of concern. Dale scoffed, "Yeah, I'm okay, I just need a minute." Alecia's anger with Gail's refusal began to dissipate. Her mind was consumed with concern as she watched Dale's fragile frame struggle to cover a distance that would have taken seconds before this horrible disease had eroded his muscle mass away.

Moments later, as Alecia contemplated checking on Dale, she was interrupted by the unwelcome presence of Kevin Kilroy. He approached her with a lecherous grin, his tone suggestive.

"Alecia," Kevin purred, "you know, you should start thinking about your future. Three years from now, he'll be long gone, a distant memory, and you're going to need someone in your life who you can depend on."

After the briefest moment of shock, Alecia's brain filled with flame. Her eyes blazed with anger, and her fists clenched at her sides. Somehow, Alecia was shocked, this insult being something that she had previously thought was beyond Kevin Kilraoy's capacity for malice. She had endured enough of his sleazy advances, and tonight was the breaking point.

Without hesitation, Alecia swung her fist, connecting squarely with Kevin's jaw. Taken by surprise. he stumbled backward, tripping over his own feet. The cocky Time Officer was shocked and disoriented, as Alecia unleashed a flurry of punches. As the startled scumbag scrambled to try to get to his feet, Alecia began kicking him mercilessly around the condo, allowing him no footing. "You sonuva bitch!" Alecia hollered, before her left combat boot once again met the officer's ribs. "You think you can come in here and say something like that?"

The party guests had watched the entire spectacle in frozen, wide-eyed shock. The commotion drew the attention of Bill Jones-Miller, who swiftly intervened. "Whoa, whoa Alecia, stop!" He grabbed Kevin by the collar, helping him to his feet, and pulling him away from Alecia's reach. "Fuckin' bitch," Kevin finally managed, blood dripping from the broken nose that she's given him and into his mouth as he spoke. "You think you can get away with this." "Shut up, Kevin," Bill said "You had too much to drink and now you're leaving. I'll walk you out." "Get out of my house you piece of shit!" Alecia spat vehemently while pointing toward the door. Kevin shot an angry, but defeated glance to Alecia before he turned away, while Bill helped him steady himself and guided him out of the door and to the waiting elevator.

As the image of Kevin disappeared behind shiny metal elevator doors, Alecia's anger began to subside, leaving her with a mix of emotions. Embarrassment, anger, concern for what the repercussions might be, concern for Dale. She turned back to the party, her heart heavy with concern.

As if on cue, Dale meekly stumbled out of the washroom. "Leesh, I'm not feelin' good." he managed, before releasing a heavy cough. Dale struggled to breathe, his vision blurring as he collapsed to the floor.

Once again, the world seemed to spin out of control for Alecia and Dale Yoshawa as they faced an uncertain future, filled with despair and desperation.

Chapter 4

The bright California sun cast a cruel contrast to the somber scene unfolding at the cemetery. Dressed in fashionable, crisp black attire, the attendees stood in silence around Dale Yoshawa's gravesite. Alecia Yoshawa, her once-vibrant spirit now shrouded in darkness, wore dark sunglasses that concealed her eyes, shielding her from the harsh reality of the moment.

Funeral attendees included familiar faces: new widow Alecia Yoshawa, Officer Kevin Kilroy, Benny Hurley, Dr. Gail Agu, Reina Yoshawa, Veronica Diegel - government liaison for Project Magenta, Franklin Morgan -senior Time Officer and colleague, and a few other Time Officers that Alecia recognized, but her memory failed to come up with their names. The Time Officers wore their formal uniforms, a symbol of the respect and brotherhood fostered by the unit. Officer Morgan's usual red mohawk had been slicked back for the event, resting on his coffee-colored skin. Liaison Officer Diegel's green eyes peeked out uncomfortably from under her blonde bangs.

Alecia's mind drifted as a priest recited passages from the Bible, the meaning of which had always escaped her. Her mind, plagued by anger and a sense of injustice, was working hard to keep reminding herself to hold it together. The day was clear and cloudless, a stark contrast to the darkness she felt within. She resented the unrelenting California sunshine, a mockery of the grief that weighed her down.

Throughout the ceremony, Alecia and Kevin Kilroy briefly exchanged icy glares on occasion. If asked, Alecia would have to admit that she was at least a little proud of the bandage on Kilroy's nose, lingering proof of the broken nose she'd given him the week before. The tension between them was palpable, a reflection of the anger and bitterness that had simmered beneath the surface for far too long.

Once the priest concluded his words, the attendees began to disperse, forming a line and offering their condolences and words of support to Alecia and Reina. Reina had lost her ability to hide her grief over her son, relying on Alecia to literally provide a shoulder to cry on several times throughout the proceedings. At least Officer Kilroy had been too busy to join the procession of condolences before leaving. After the rest of the attendees had dispersed, Alecia soberly made her way to her car. She held herself together long enough to leave the cemetery, her expression a mask of stoicism. But as soon as she was alone in her flying car, strapped into her 5-point harness, the floodgates of grief burst open, and she sobbed uncontrollably. Alecia, who loved driving, for the first time, had to allow the autopilot to take her all the way home.

In the weeks that followed, Alecia sank deeper into a pit of despair. She stopped going to work at Project Magenta, unable to face the reminders of Dale that lingered in every corner of the facility. To cope with her loss and mourning, she began drinking heavily and smoking a lot of weed, seeking solace in the haze of intoxication.

When Alecia was able to suppress her grief long enough to sleep, her nights were filled with haunting dreams, where Dale appeared by her side, assuring her he had never died. But each morning, she awoke to the harsh reality that he was gone, the emotional pain cutting twice as deep as before.

On one particular night, after smoking a joint and passing out on the couch, she was awoken by the sound of the door of the condo opening, pouring light across her startled and sleep-addled mind. It was Dale, in full military police uniform. He was fit and looked to be in the prime of his life. "Honey, I'm home!" he said cheerily. Alecia couldn't believe it. She knew she'd fallen asleep on the couch, but could not understand how her dead husband could be there. "What, no...Dale you died," Alecia half-murmured, still fighting the extreme fatigue caused by sleepless grief. "Honey, no, no, I'm right here. You just had a bad dream." Alecia didn't have the strength to make sense of it anymore, as Dale sat on the couch next to her she fell sobbing into his chest, wrapping her arms around him.

The hug caused her arms to move involuntarily, the sensation quickly bringing Alecia to consciousness. She quickly looked around the dark, empty apartment. Another dream. Alecia released a roar of frustration as she tossed an empty whiskey bottle, once sitting on the coffee table, against the wall. Glass shattered in cacophony compared to the rest of the quiet apartment. She was angry that there was no escape from the grief she felt, even in her own mind, her own dreams.

Alecia, still in a half-alcohol and marijuana-induced haze, found herself on the streets of Los Angeles. She wandered past dance clubs, 3-D arcades, fetish bars, and hot dog vendors with barely an acknowledgment. Her grief-fueled wanderings found her standing at a familiar gray building. She looked up at the facade and security gate of Project Magenta. Alecia had a moment to consider that maybe this had been her destination all along. "Fuckin' right," she muttered, pulling her alpha-level security card from her wallet. She may have been away from work on bereavement for the last week, but her security card was still active. She swiped the card, smiled at the retinal scan, and gave a drunken smile to the confused security guard as she passed through the gate. In the middle of the night, she entered the facility, driven by an overwhelming need to see Dale again. She knew that the security desk would be notified that an employee had scanned in without being scheduled for duty. She knew that the building was tracking her, a moving dot on a screen, and that a friendly member of the security team would be coming to ask her if she needed help with something in less than 5 minutes.

As she moved through the corridors, purposely avoiding the usual patrol points of the security team, the building's security computer noticed her evasive behavior. Silent, spinning lights slowly began extruding from panels in the walls, making sure everyone in the building was aware that there was a low-level security threat on the premises. Alecia knew that security would be scrambling, and would find her sooner or later. With several corridors to pass before she got to the locker room, Alecia broke into a sprint. Panic alarms began to blare, the warning light turning from orange to red, and security personnel rushed into the corridor behind her to investigate the intrusion. Alecia's heart raced as she heard their approaching footsteps. "Hey, Stop!" the largest black man Alecia had ever seen, a Security Officer of seven and a half feet tall, if he was an inch, bellowed, his voice echoing in cacophony in the sterile corridor.

Alecia cleared the locker room and approached the entrance to the engine room in about three seconds. Chasing Alecia through the labyrinthine building had already put the Security Officers pursuing her at a disadvantage. They were clearly not as familiar with the civilian locker room as Alecia, proven by the slowing bottleneck of guards navigating around the banks of lockers, fervently searching for the intruder. With the reality of the fact that she was breaking into one of the most heavily secured government labs in the world, panic gripped her, but she was determined to reach the one place that held the key to changing everything.

Alecia's furious speed propelled her across the engine room, only to come to a sudden stop when she was confronted by something unexpected that she had hoped wouldn't happen. She found herself cornered by Dr. Gail Agu, who sternly stood blocking the entrance to the Time Lab. "No Alecia, you are not doing this!" Gail said sternly. Alecia's burgeoning hope was crushed. Alecia was overcome with emotion. First, there was anger, and for a brief second, she had considered punching her friend right in the face. The horror of her own thoughts and behavior hit her like a truck and she began to break down. "I can't do it. I can't live without him Gail, I can't, I can't do it" Alecia stammered, knees beginning to wobble under her. Gail's heart cried for the emotional wreck that her friend had become. She whispered, "Push me over and run." "What?" Alecia said, having trouble comprehending Gail's words and processing her own emotional trauma at the same time. The large security guard from earlier was striding toward them across the engine room. "This lady's gonna get the book thrown at her," the towering stack of muscles mumbled to himself.

In response to her friend's slowness, Gail huffed and dramatically threw herself to the floor, giving Alecia a wide-eyed "get moving" expression, as she began to flail dramatically. Alecia only had a split second to register the shock of what her friend had just done before her legs took over, propelling her toward the Time Well platform. Alecia's hands scrambled desperately, flipping switches and hitting buttons that brought control consoles to life. Alecia stole a glance over her shoulder, where Gail had been doing her best impression of a helplessly flailing and distressed senior, who just happened to be slowing the progress of the big burly Security Officer. The guard finally pushed past her, trailed by 12 more members of the security detail. Alecia pressed a large round plunger that triggered the powering up of the Time Well. She thought to herself about what she knew of the time sciences. One of the primary things that were understood to be true was that the distance traveled backward was in direct proportion to the momentum at which the subject was moving when they entered the Time Well. She took a quick look at some of the metal paneled rigging that the console equipment was mounted on. Without time to think, she climbed a panel of metal grating until she was perched, clinging to the metal lattice, about 5 feet above the tallest monitor screen on the console. The security team was flanking either side of the control platform, the big man who'd been eager to see her punished to the full extent of the law walked onto the platform, hands outstretched. "Okay lady, I don't know what you think you're achieving, but it's time to come down and stop this."

The guard's puzzled statement reminded Alecia of why she had stormed this lab in the first place. The memory of Dale's smiling face flashed in her mind. With one final glance back at the world she was leaving behind, Alecia hurled herself into the rippling pink waves of time, disappearing into the unknown.

Chapter 5

Alecia's eyes fluttered open, and she found herself in a world she thought she had left behind forever. She was a child again, lying in her small, familiar bedroom. Panic welled up inside her as she realized that she had traveled back too far, to a time shortly after the death of her mother, June. The room was filled with the soft glow of the morning sun, and the memories of her past came rushing back.

Blinking away the disorientation, Alecia pushed back the covers and climbed out of bed. She padded across the room in her pajamas and looked out the window, recognizing the view of their suburban neighborhood. It was a bittersweet sensation, being back here again, her heart swelled with conflicting nostalgia at the chance to see her father, Brian, once more.

Excitement and trepidation churned in her stomach as she descended the stairs. The familiar sounds of her childhood home filled her ears—the creaking of wooden steps, the distant hum of the television, and the faint smell of coffee brewing in the kitchen.

As she entered the kitchen, her heart skipped a beat. There he was— the imposing form of her father, Brian Hernandez, hunched over the kitchen table, sipping a cup of coffee. His face was etched with a mix of weariness and sorrow, a reflection of the emotional pain and inner turmoil he had endured since his wife's tragic accident, still freshly in the recent past for him.

"Daddy?" Alecia's voice wavered as she approached him, her adult mind still struggling to accept the reality of being in her childhood body, reliving the past.

Brian looked up, his tired eyes widening in surprise as he saw his daughter. "'Lecia? M...Morning honey. Did you sleep okay?" His voice quivered with the raw emotion of the troubled thoughts that his daughter interrupted.

Tears welled up in Alecia's eyes as she embraced her father, relishing the warmth of his love. "...Daddy," she whispered, her voice choked with emotion and she breathed in the familiar scent of sweat and English Leather aftershave that she'd been missing for years, though she knew she could never voice her feelings out loud in this time.

"Hey now honey...it's going to be okay." Brian Henandez choked out, trying to set a brave example through his own sorrow. "...I know it's been hard since your mom..." the immense man couldn't bring himself to finish the thought. "But you and I are going to get through this. If you need to talk, if you need anything, you can come to me any time."

"Yes, Daddy." Alecia buried her head in the big man's shoulder, letting tears flow into the short-sleeved navy work shirt with his name embroidered on the left side of his chest, unable to explain or even process the full range of emotions that had brought her tears on.

The day stretched before them, and Alecia spent it with her father, cherishing every moment. They talked about everything and nothing, reminiscing about old times and sharing their dreams for the future. Brian taught her about how catalytic converters in old cars worked, something that she showed an aptitude for, thanks to the experience of her adult mind, in a way that took even her father by surprise. Alecia had forgotten just how much she had enjoyed the carefree simplicity of being a child. She enjoyed and absorbed every moment she could with her father. The smell of spent engine oil and orange-scented scrub, for getting all manner of machine fluids off of your hands, stirred a deep and abiding nostalgia in Alecia. She watched with fascination as he tinkered with the engine of an old car in their garage, his hands deftly spinning ratchets and wrenches, removing and replacing an assortment of parts.

Her mothers old music files played on the wall mounted speakers. At one point Alecia had begun singing along, and they both experienced a rush of somber emotion when P!NK's "Who Knew?", a favorite of her mothers, came on. The irony of how the song's lyrics stirred similarities to, what to Brian was the recent loss of her mother, though neither said it out loud.

In a moment of awkward silence, Alecia decided to say something that she hadn't had the experience to say during her first time around as a child. "You know it's not your fault, right dad?" Brian Hernandez froze in the middle of tightening an engine bolt, then looked up silently at his daughter, tears welling in his eyes. "I can't help but think...maybe if I'd run another diagnostic check on the autopilot...or changed the glow plugs sooner..." The big mechanic allowed his daughter to embrace him, switching roles this time, his tears seeping into the pink pajamas that she hadn't bothered to change out of. "It's not your fault Daddy. It's no one's fault, there's nothing anyone could have done."

As the day drew to a close, Alecia tried to suggest things about the future without revealing too much, knowing that altering the past could have unforeseen consequences. She speculated about moving to the city when she was older, maybe to take a heavy equipment mechanics course, carefully framing it as a hypothetical scenario. Brian shared advice on pursuing her dreams and told her to follow her heart. "Honey, you can be a mechanic or an astronaut or the president, as long as you're happy, and I'll always be here to help you." Alecia felt a pang of sorrow that she struggled to keep from showing on her face, knowing that his promise of support was well-intentioned, but would not be possible.

That night, as Alecia lay in her childhood bed, she reached for her diary, hidden beneath her mattress. With trembling hands, she began to write a message to her future self. She scrawled "Research Time Travel, it's going to be important in the FUTURE!!" She knew that she could not explain the full details, for fear of causing damage to the future or making her younger self look insane.

With her message completed, Alecia closed the diary and set it aside. Exhaustion washed over her, and she drifted off to sleep, hoping that her message would guide her on the path to rewriting history and securing a future with the love of her life.

Chapter 6

Alecia tumbled out of the Time Well, her heart pounding in her chest. She half-expected to be surrounded by Time Force security forces, ready to apprehend her for her unauthorized time jump. However, to her surprise, the scene before her was entirely different.

Instead of stern-faced officers, she was met by a familiar face, Dr. Gail Agu, who greeted her with a warm smile. "Officer Hernandez, it's good to see you back," Dr. Agu said, her tone filled with genuine warmth.

Alecia's mind raced. "Don't you mean Mechanic Yoshawa?" she replied, thoroughly confused by the use of her maiden name in Gail's greeting, something that she was long since used to hearing, since she chose to take Dale's name when they married.

Dr. Agu's brow furrowed. "I'm not sure what you mean,". A look of sudden realization crossed the doctor's face and she chuckled, "Oh, I get it, you're trying to say that we couldn't do this without the grunts,". "We do have a great team of mechanics," she added, giving an amused nod to some workers visible through the opening to the engine room in the distance. "Great work, guys!" Gail shouted. In the distance, a pair of confused mechanics stopped their work, giving a confused look at the shout of acknowledgment. One was clearly Benny, though his safety helmet had a custom airbrush painting of a flaming phoenix on it. "I'll have to ask him where he got that done!" Alecia thought to herself. The other mechanic gave an awkward, unsure wave. His expression gave the impression that he had likely not entirely heard or understood the message, by the time the sound had reached the task-focused workers in the engine room.

And then Alecia realized that it was Dale.

It was Dale, but not the Dale that she knew. He looked more haggard than Dale had been in his prime. Bags under his eyes, maybe a few more wrinkles. He didn't necessarily look older, but as if he hadn't aged well, as if a number of untold events had taken a heavier toll on him than Alecia was used to seeing. Where the Dale she knew had kept his hair short since joining the Time Force, this person, this Dale, had long hair pulled into a ponytail. Loose, that hair could have easily reached the middle of his back. Where Alecia was used to seeing Dale clean-shaven, this Dale had bushy sideburns and a scraggly soul patch, surrounded by several days worth of stubble covering the rest of the beard area of his face. The Dale before her was unrecognizable— not just because of scruffy, long hair. It was his subdued personality that seemed to have paid the toll of all of Alecia's changes to time. He nearly looked like a completely different person, and not the confident Time Officer she knew and loved. Her heart ached at the sight of him, but she couldn't reveal the truth about their past. Slowly, a realization that Alecia did not want to accept grew in her mind. Slowly, she looked down, and in repressed terror, she realized that the coveralls that she expected herself to be wearing had been replaced by a padded time-jump suit.

Alecia's heart sank as she realized that her message in her diary had indeed altered history. She was now a Time Officer, and Dale, her beloved Dale, was a mechanic. "How could this have happened?" Alecia thought to herself, still processing a dual set of memories, one which would hold the answer to how she had lived her life in this timeline. In a flurry of conflicting emotions, Alecia struggled to suppress the terror she was feeling in her mind from showing in her expression. Dr. Agu,was still standing there, staring at her, attempting to discuss upcoming debrief details.

Alecia fought to suppress nausea and a painful ball of anxiety in her stomach, as her new memories forced her to accept the reality that she was now in, where she had chosen to focus on her education and career, and broke up with Dale after they had completed high school.

They were not married or together, and her entire reality had shifted.

All this, and still Alecia knew that she had to present a calm and professional demeanor, even in front of her friend Gale, because she could not afford to answer questions that would prove her guilty of abusing one of society's primary time laws.

"Leesh? Are you ok? Did you hit your head down there? We really should reconsider getting helmets for you guys..." Dr. Agu said, fishing around her lab coat pocket for a penlight she planned to use to check Alecia's pupils.

Alecia swallowed hard, pushing down a thousand new anxieties that her time jump had created, waving off Gail's tiny flashlight she put on a brave face, "Yes, yes I'm okay," she lied, "Just had a moment there...integrating some new memories...I'll save it for the Time Directors." The pair had already begun moving toward the expected debrief room.

"Don't let him hear you say that," Gail said with a sideways smile. Alecia had a moment of realization. The panel of nine Time Directors that she had been familiar with in her original timeline had been replaced several years ago, by one person, in this one.

Alecia was quickly ushered into a debriefing by Dr. Agu. The large burgundy room with warm lighting and a large, horseshoe-shaped table that could seat 10-12 people that Alecia had been expecting, was gone. In its place, was a small room, no bigger than twelve by twelve feet, with black walls and stark lighting. Half the room was occupied by a large desk, nearly splitting the room in half. Behind the desk sat General Charles Andrews, a Time Director that she'd been familiar with in her original timeline. This version of General Andrews had the same "not-aged-well" look that the new version of Dale had. His face was paler, with deeper lines and wrinkles, jowls bigger, his body chubbier, and his Chestnut hair held wisps of gray that his previous counterpart hadn't had. Two basic, steel-framed chairs nearly filled the open space on Gail and Alecia's side of the desk.

"Did you meet the mission objectives, Officer?" the Time Director asked, before Alecia had finished seating herself in the chair closest to the door. "We had some unusual energy spikes in your chronal discharge charts." Her mind was still catching up with new memories. What had felt like a vague memory was slowly solidifying, in this Timeline, she'd been working a case, to give a young biology major's idea a little nudge, which would help him to go on to become the professor who developed enhanced urban produce growing methods. Alecia knew that the "spike" in the charts had likely been caused by the fact that she had traveled much further back in time than the mission objectives had expected, thanks to the high climb she'd made before jumping, but she couldn't very well tell him that. Alecia met the Time Director's stern gaze. "Y...yes."

She struggled to navigate the conversation, afraid that she would somehow reveal her manipulation of the past. She carefully crafted her responses, blending truths with half-truths, and giving the details she thought they wanted to hear. As far as they knew, her assignment to be overheard by a young genius went swimmingly.

Just as Alecia thought her mind would crack, half expecting a burly security guard to bust through the wall and point at her accusingly, revealing her time-altering machinations, that Time Director looked at the pink-haired time traveler, "Good work Officer, that will be all." he stated matter-of-factly. "Dr. Agu please stay and discuss the charts with me, and see if we may need to run some diagnostics."

Alecia blinked, relieved to be done with the most intense interview she'd had in her life, she raced the other two people in the room to stand and quickly stammered "Thank you sir." before getting herself the hell out of that claustrophobic room.

"Hey, partner!" a voice came from behind Alecia before she could get more than fifteen feet down the corridor leading back to the Time Officer locker room.

In this altered reality, Kevin Kilroy was a constant presence, not just aggressively pursuing Alecia and ignoring her repeated rejections, but also assigned as her partner Time Officer in this timeline.

"I'm sure that it wasn't too hard to get that nerd's attention for you, was it?" Kilroy's lecherous gaze held an uncomfortably long and steady eye contact, as he flexed his eyebrows suggestively.

"You know that's not how we complete objectives, *Officer* Kilroy." Alecia's flat response carried palpable disdain. Her pace hadn't slowed a bit, leaving her partner scrambling to keep up. "Yeah, but come on!" Kilroy had latched on and wouldn't let go. "It's gotta be easier for someone as **HOT** as you, to get these geeks to listen to you." Alecia ignored Kilroy's statement, weaving her way toward the bank of lockers that her new memories were familiar with, without ever making eye contact with her pursuer.

Alecia allowed the small laser emitted from her locker's door scanner to slowly shine a line of red light across her retina. The door popped open with a "click" sound. As Alecia began organizing to change into her civilian clothes, Officer Kilroy, still hovering around her like a bee desperate for attention, casually leaned sideways on the door of the locker next to hers, facing her. She kept looking straight ahead, continuing to try to ignore him.

"It's been a long day "Leesh", whadda you say we make today the day that we finally share a mutual shower session? There's plenty of room in those stalls you know..." Kilroy's advances were interrupted, much to his shock, as Alecia's hands firmly grabbed either side of his collar, pushing him backward and slamming his back into the hard steel of the opposite bank of lockers before he could plant his feet in resistance. Alecia had finally had enough of this dickhead. She didn't hold back, shaking the surprised pervert and slamming him against the cold steel again, a metal door hinge painfully digging into his back. "FUCK OFF!" she screamed into his face, before roughly slapping him in the side of the head several times in frustration and kneeing him in the balls.

Doubled over in pain, Kevin was not in any position to offer a defense. Alecia's fingers grabbed the hair on the back of her partner's head, pulling back hard as she leaned forward to angrily whisper to him through gritted teeth. "If you ever make a comment like that again, if you so much as look at me in a way that I don't like, I will make sure everyone in this facility and your life, knows that you lost your precious job as a Time Officer for sexual harassment." Alecia seethed, nearly spitting out her words. "You will respect my boundaries, Officer!"

"Everything okay here?" Senior Time Officer Morgan had entered the locker room just as Alecia had released her grip on Officer Kilroy. "Yes, he's just not feeling well." Alecia stated anger still giving an edge to her voice. She briskly strode past the senior officer toward the shower stall, civilian clothes in hand. "Too many strip club chicken wings, wasn't it?" Kilroy and Alecia exchanged a glare, neither apparently feeling the need to hide their animosity from the senior officer in the room. "Yes." Kilroy painfully muttered from his hunched position.

"Good!" Officer Morgan intoned, turning his attention away. "I got too much goddamn paperwork to do as it is!"

Alecia was already locking a shower stall as Morgan strode away to his own locker, leaving Kilroy to nurse his aching testicles.

Alecia couldn't help but let the tense encounter with Kilroy and the loss of her relationship with Dale play on her mind, making it difficult to enjoy the warm water running down her body, in what would normally have been a relaxing shower. Alecia dressed in the shower stall, not wanting to risk being in a vulnerable state around her own investigative partner. She was pleased to see that he was gone when she returned to her locker. She knew that he had likely worn his Time Officer uniform home, so he could squeeze out just a bit more of that feeling of power and authority into his day.

She peeked into the engine room long enough to see that Dale wasn't present. He'd likely finished his shift for the day.

Alecia passed through a security gate and took the elevator up to the rooftop parking docks. Her pink hover car had been replaced with a military police car in this timeline. She missed her little pink airbug, but she couldn't argue that this armored 4-seater had some incredible gadgets, primarily, the video screen console where a Time Officer could access not only anything on the civilian info-web, but secured information, housed on the Time Force mainframe. Literally, anything that might help a Time Officer investigate a case.

Alecia thought of the pale shadow of the person she had known as "her" Dale. A shadow she'd somehow created with a simple message in a journal.

She couldn't let it stand. Against her better judgment, as her car lifted vertically from the roof docking bay, Alecia began accessing the Project Magenta civilian employee files. It turned out that although she still had the same address as the old timeline, Dale had a different address, in a place across town that she wasn't sure she'd ever visited before. She double-tapped the address on the screen, informing the car navigation system that this was its new destination. The car quickly ascended vertically, the onboard computers constantly scanning and recalculating for the swiftest route. As the car rose, it made a smooth gradual arc, increasing forward thrust as the upward thrust lowered, making a smooth transition, keeping the human inside of the flying tin can as comfortable and jostle free as possible. Autopilot quickly propelled the military vehicle through the air above the city. Alecia rarely allowed vehicles to fly themselves, that is what took her mother, after all, but this time, she allowed the machine to plot its course, engrossed in the data she had found on **THIS** version of Dale.

It looked like this version Dale was still a UC Berkeley classmate, but their majors had switched, with Dale being a star pupil in Time Travel Mechanics, until his final year at least. His grades dropped, and it looked like he must have fallen in with the wrong crowd, an assumption from the low-level Narcotics possession charge. Dale's grades were so good and he was still so smart that it didn't affect his ability to graduate and apply to the civilian branch of Project Magenta. Lucky for him, his second application had been accepted before he'd had time to stack up more charges. Nothing big at first. A couple of unpaid parking tickets, drunk and disorderly, then a few DUIs. Alecia released an exasperated huff at the thought that the Dale she knew could be stupid enough to drive under the influence. The DUIs had cost him his license, he started taking public transit to work after that, then he was caught with a major amount of heroin, charged with intent to distribute. Alecia was horrified that this version of Dale could be so different from the one she knew. A led ball of guilt sat in the pit of her stomach. She blamed herself. Somehow, her decision to try to save him, or was it when she chose to "focus on herself"?, had affected Dale's life in some way that led to him harboring a serious heroin addiction. At least that was the argument that Project Magenta-provided lawyers said, having him plead to a lesser charge and agree to attend a rehab facility, which his excellent Project Magenta employee benefits would pay for.

It looked like Dale had been out of rehab and back on the job for nearly a year now.

Alecia looked up from the info on her data screen and finally began to take in her surroundings.

The car's engines had quieted, shifting into hover mode as it lowered itself from its sky-high vantage point into this version of Dale's neighborhood. It slowly worked its way above streets and between buildings, a crawling search toward its destination. Alecia was startled into silence by what she saw. Filth, garbage and graffiti seemed to grow like moss from the streets and alleys and up the walls, on dilapidated buildings with boarded up windows and heavily barred doorways.

Alecia had never come to this part of town before, but she knew it had never been like this, not in her original timeline anyway. Where she came from, the work of the Time Force had all but eliminated poverty and famine. Clearly, in this timeline, they were behind on some of those goals.

The police car slowly lowered itself onto a gravel patch in front of a small rundown looking apartment building, clad in deteriorating brown wood shingles. The second floor of the three story building sported a large balcony, enclosed by metal panels that had been painted an unflattering aqua colour, now faded and peeling with time. The balcony was decorated with a clothes line, haphazardly strung from a bolt screwed into the building, in the frame surrounding the outside of a sliding glass patio door, the other end tied to a metal bar that ran above the green-blue metal paneling. An assortment of dirty and broken children's toys were strewn about, between equally haggard pieces of patio furniture. One corner seemed to be the home of a pile of household items that were being held on to, though if she was being honest, Alecia thought they looked like they could be taken to a dump and not be missed.

The whole scene puzzled Alecia. How had this become where Dale had lived? Even with the Time Force dropping the ball on fighting poverty AND Dale's run-ins with the law, it seemed that Project Magenta still paid very well. So how had this become Dale's fate? The thoughts stirred an unpleasant stew of guilt, remorse and other unsavory feelings in the pit of Alecia's stomach.

As she exited the car, a beautiful, but tired looking, black woman, holding a child that looked to be about a year old on her hip, opened that sliding glass door and stepped onto the balcony. The mystery woman shot a cold, analytical look at the car and its occupant as she gripped the edge of a peeling metal panel with her free hand.

Before Alecia could get her bearings and formulate an actual plan of what she was going to say to this version of Dale, the woman on the balcony harshly interrupted her thought process. "Y'all lookin' for Dale?" the woman asked in a stern, suspicious tone. Momentarily surprised at her luck, Alecia responded brightly, "Yes...Yes I am."

The woman on the balcony was not impressed. "Well I knew it was a matter of time before someone came lookin' for him again. What's he done this time?" the woman asked flatly, setting down her baby in a dilapidated chair so that she could light a cigarette. "No, no, he hasn't done anything. I...I'm a...co-worker, and I'm here to talk to him about something..." "Ha!" the women on the balcony laughed bitterly, "You're a "co-worker", lookin' to talk? You must have fallen for some of his shit honey, but sorry, he ain't here. I kicked his ass out at least a month ago now." Alecia was taken aback. Could this woman be his landlord? Whether she was or not, she didn't have much choice but to try and use the resources at hand and press for more information. "Do...you have any idea where I could find him?" she asked the clearly stressed and agitated woman on the balcony. "No, but if you're lookin' for 'im, you might wanna try the nearest crack house!" the woman shouted.

The rising volume of the woman's voice drew more children from the balcony's sliding door. They silently walked over to the woman, framing her on either side. On the left was a girl, of about nine years, wearing a dirty floral print dress, her brown hair was long and matted, running down the full length of her back. The girl's skin was a coffee coloured blend of her mother's and whoever her father was. On the right, a boy of about six, wearing a set of flannel onesie pajamas that was as equally as dirty as his sister's. The child had the same complexion as his older sister, but there was no doubt of his parentage. He looked timidly out at Alecia with Dale's eyes. Alecia finally made the realization that the woman was not Dale's landlord, but his lover. She was experiencing stunned silence a lot for one day.

"Well, you do me a favor," the woman continued, "If you find him, you ask him why he thinks it's okay to snort and shoot up all that money that y'all are payin' him instead of supportin' his kids."

The woman suppressed her own tears as she flicked the ash from her cigarette onto the concrete pad of the balcony, then pulled her children closer.

Alecia's mind swirled. It seemed that this timeline held a fresh new horror every time that she turned around. She couldn't speak. Her stomach churned as she reached for the still-open car door. "I'm...I'm sorry to have bothered you ma'am." Alecia managed. "Ha!" the woman responded bitterly. "I'm sure you are. Good luck, *honey*."

Alecia sat staring at the car's dashboard, wishing she'd taken the time to read more details about this version of Dale before she'd tried to contact him. She felt sick, overcome with guilt, knowing that this dark timeline had been the result of her actions. She felt stupid. Time Travel had been restricted for a reason. "You're so stupid! You made everything worse!", she thought to herself, choking back the heavy sobs that wanted to leave her body. She needed a distraction. She turned the car on, avoiding the icy glare still coming from the woman on the balcony surrounded by confused children. She disengaged the autopilot and grabbed the driving bar. In times like this she needed to drive. The car lifted until it was just above the roof level of the three-story building, and an icy gaze continued to follow it. Alecia pulled the bar toward her and to the right, steering the armored car into flying street traffic. She pressed the accelerator, telling the high-tech flying tank to increase its velocity to the 85KM/H residential zone speed limit. She explored the unfamiliar slums of Los Angeles looking for answers. Looking for something. Looking for Dale. Looking for the man that she'd changed history for. A man that she may never see again.

She watched the people of the slums scurrying like meth-fueled ants. Tents filled with homeless people lined the streets on either side, crowding entrances to apartment buildings and businesses and congesting the human foot traffic of the street. Some tents sported hand-scrawled signs pinned to a canopy, competing with local businesses for goods and services, some offering more illicit substances. The people walking the streets and coming in and out of buildings didn't look much better off than the tent dwellers that they had to squeeze between in order to run daily errands. Everyone was some level of looking unwashed. No one wore a piece of clothing that looked new, or didn't have a fray or tatter somewhere. For those of the downtrodden that still bothered to look up, their gaze locked on the gliding vehicle, quickly finishing whatever illicit activity was in progress upon the familiar sight of a military police vehicle.

Alecia noticed a very distressed and strung out looking woman, a spiky blue mohawk waving in the air complemented with a shiny silver chain that ran from her left nostril to earlobe, dotted with a small diamond stud on each end, stumble from a dilapidated tenement and collapse onto a rare open space on the sidewalk. The woman's eyes rolled back and she went into convulsions. The movement of human traffic continued uninterrupted, as if a person hadn't just collapsed and begun flailing in their midst.

Alecia hurriedly pushed the stick forward bringing the vehicle downward, the force of the wind from the armored hovercar forced the humans below to make an opening big enough for the vehicle to squeeze into for a landing. Alecia grabbed her badge and flashlight and ran from the vehicle toward the tattered looking woman, writhing and foaming at the mouth. Alecia quickly removed her sweater, balling it up and placing it under the woman's head as a pillow, then helped roll her to the side, gently guiding her body into a position where she was less likely to choke. She pulled out the officer's standard issue penlight that she'd grabbed from the vehicle before her mad dash to save a stranger. She shone the light into large, black, unreactive pupils. "I'm here to help," Alecia said into the blank expression. "What did you take? What's your name?" In response the woman gagged hard and blew a mouthful of vomit onto the ground next to them, continuing to convulse and foam with no sign of being mentally present.

Alecia looked up and stared in bewilderment at the people coming and going around them, with no hint or acknowledgement of the dramatic situation occurring on the street around them. "What's wrong with you people," Alecia shouted at the equally non-responsive pedestrians. "Can't you see she needs help? Someone get help!" "I can help you." A middle aged man with sagging jowls in a floor length trench coat and fedora stepped out of the indifferent masses, locking eyes as he moved toward Alecia. "Sounds like you and your friend need some Narcan."

"Yes!" Alecia stammered. "Do you have any?" "57 Creds." the man replied flatly. "What?" Alecia replied in wide-eyed disbelief. "I'm trying to save this person's life!" "And I'm offering you the police discount," the man gestured with a nod toward Alecia's parked vehicle. "So I guess we're both doin' our good deed for the day." Apparently the indifferent masses noticed a lot more than they let on. Alecia seethed in frustration at the desperation of her situation. "God, there's no time for this!" she exclaimed through gritted teeth as she grabbed for the payment device that she knew would be embedded in her belt. Without having to look she pulled a small red light framed with a little plastic box, about the size of her thumbnail from her right hip and pulled it toward the trench coat clad man. The device was attached to a thin, spring loaded cable, designed to pull it back into place after use, like a security guard's keychain. The mysterious man pulled a similar device from his belt and moved toward Alecia. She held her device, hovering over his and both lights turned green with a small "beep" noise. The man released his device, allowing it to flail as it loudly retracted back to his belt. As the payment device found its home, a button in the middle of his trenchcoat glowed yellow, making a noise like a large vault being unlocked. Grabbing the button, the man jerked his coat open. Alecia was taken aback by the swift motion, and then the startling image it revealed. The man's jacket was lined with a shiny metal material and featured rows of illicit substances for sale. Weed, some kind of pills, heroin, meth, and one row of Narcan injectable canisters. Next to the contraband the left side of the man's body was revealed. Shockingly, his shirtless hairy torso matched the chubby, sagging look of his face. Thankfully, he was wearing something, however minimal, below his waist. A spiked leather belt matched a black leather brief with matching garter belts, running to a pair of five-inch stilettos. Alecia had no time to process the absurdity of the situation as the man pulled the canister she'd paid for from his jacket and handed it to her. "Her ya go, pleasure doin' business witcha'!"

An angry "huff" was her only response as her attention turned back to the woman on the ground. The pool of vomit next to her had grown larger, but there was no movement. The woman's body was eerily still, her gaze wide-eyed and empty as foam dried into a crust on her lips. Alecia pressed her fingers into the woman's neck, though she knew already that there wasn't a pulse to be found there. She looked back to the man she'd just bought the Narcan from, but he was gone, melded into the throng of indifferent, unwashed masses. She returned her gaze to the woman, desperately beginning chest compressions in futility. She angrily punched the deceased woman's chest, teeth clenched in frustration, fighting the sorrow she felt inside. Still unsure of her next step Alecia stood, sliding the Narcan into her pocket as she rose. She looked down, looked around, and looked up at the drug den that the woman had stumbled out from. "Are you plannin's to take this?" the voice of an elderly homeless woman, her clothes a patchwork of tatters, interrupted Alecia's observations. "What? No!" she responded with irritation, as the woman gestured to the sparkling stud on the woman's nose. "Well then you shouldn't care if I do." the woman responded matter-of-factly, fingerless gloved hands already working to loosen the clasp inside the dead woman's nostril.

Aghast, Alecia was so horrified that she hadn't managed to shout for this ghoul to get away before more opportunists joined the scene. "This lady really don't want this stuff? Rich people I guess..." one man mumbled as his hands began checking the dead woman's pockets. The small child, whose hand he'd been holding, maybe walking home from school, moved around over the woman's head. A young girl of no more than four years looked up, smiling in thanks to Alecia, then returned to her work, silently unclasping the dead woman's spiked leather collar and pocketing it, in just a few, very quick, very well practiced motions.

While Alecia silently backed away in horror, she looked away from the scene and back to the drug den. "Well, she said to check the nearest crackhouse." Alecia thought, making the best of her experience with this version of Dale's baby momma.

The drugden was one of the last single family homes still standing within the city limits of Los Angeles. It had once been a two family dwelling, a large house with two semi-detached units, but the new tenants had long since smashed holes in the dividing walls where necessary, to increase space for more mattresses and cushions for stoners to flop on while they enjoyed their euphoria.

Alecia marched into the open door of the home and was immediately hit with a putrid mix that smelled like cat urine and vomit. What passed for a living room had a dingy, stain streaked, well-worn gray rug floor that had probably been white at one time. People in various states of consciousness were strewn about like debris, along with blankets, vomit, garbage and needles. Alecia stepped into the room slowly, eyes moving constantly to scan for any sign of Dale or of danger. She swallowed hard, doing her best not to breathe in enough for the acrid stench to make her gag. A form stepped forward from the dark edges of the room. "Whatcha want?" a haggard-looking man of about 40, in a stained undershirt and denim shorts held up by suspenders stepped forward, Alecia had been so distracted by the smell, that she'd missed the glow of the large joint the man had clenched in his teeth.

After a moment of hesitation, Alecia decided to play things cool "I'm just looking for someone." she said matter-of-factly, but as she went to step forward, the man's arm slid down in front of her like a pay parking gate, the back of his hand pressing uncomfortably hard into the middle of her chest. "You shoot here, you buy here." The man's face held a stern impression, suggesting that he was already unimpressed with the fact that he'd had to state the rule for Alecia. A large, serious looking dark skinned man moved from a partially obscured position in the kitchen to fill the frame of the kitchen door, silently backing up the man glaring at Alecia. Apparently the big guy that had been chasing Alecia when she time-jumped, had found a different career in this timeline. "Heh," Alecia feigned laughter. "No, really, I'm just looking for someone." Alecia pressed forward, but the man's hand refused to yield. "Listen lady, just get outta here." the suspendered man said. "It's bad enough I gotta replace a wife now, but I don't mind harvesting organs from two bodies, if I have to."

Alecia responded by grabbing the man's index finger with one hand, and forearm with the other, pulling his finger in the wrong direction and twisting his arm, forcing him to his knees with a painful cry. The military training that Alecia had gotten from the memories of this timeline were proving quite useful. The dark behemoth in the kitchen barreled toward Alecia like a freight train. Alecia gripped the man's wrist behind his back, freeing up a hand to hold out the Time Force badge she'd slipped into her pocket while in the car, and show it to the man mountain bearing down on her. The man suddenly stumbled sideways in surprise, but managed to keep moving forward. His eyes were wide with fear. "You're a cop?" the man asked aloud to the room. "Fuck, shit, sorry Bill!" the man stammered, picking up his pace and running out the open door. "That's what I thought!" Alecia proclaimed, proud that her gamble had paid off.

"I'm sorry, I'm sorry, I didn't know you were a cop! I'm sorry!" the man on the floor, his arm still being very much wrenched behind his back. "Look, Bill..." Alecia started, before the features of the man's face finally came into focus in her mind. This was the man she'd known as

Bill Jones-Miller. In this reality, he seemed to be the proprietor of this drug den. "Get out of here," Alecia seethed. "R...really?" Bill questioned in confusion. Bill was smart enough to be scrambling for the door by the time an angry Alecia shouted "Get out!"

Alecia slowly explored each room, working cautiously with her penlight pointed ahead, ready to kick someone's ass if she needed to. She examined the faces of people passed out on the decaying couches and cushions. Some covered their eyes, grunting their frustration, others looked up languidly from their position, draped across another person, completely passed out. As she entered the second upstairs bedroom she noticed a handgun laying on the floor. Alecia thought it had likely fallen out of the waistband of the man who lay on the floor, snoring on his side. Without taking her eyes off the sleeping man, she slowly bent down and reached for the gun. She examined it gingerly with her fingers, then pressed the button that released the ammo cartridge. Almost a full clip. Alecia decided she'd hang on to that gun and pointed it in front of her, beside the flashlight. The former owner continued to snore as she stepped past him.

Though she checked every corner, Alecia felt defeated, finding no signs of Dale. 30 minutes after she entered, a dejected Alecia exited the crooked, sagging wooden porch that hung limply from the front of the house. Alecia was torn with grief. The more she learned about the world that her actions had created, the worse it got. She couldn't help looking toward the dead woman that she'd tried to save just a short time ago, a mix of guilt and morbid curiosity tugging at her eyes. The body was still there, but had now been stripped down to her underwear. Even her long, blue hair had been taken, shorn off by some unseen opportunist who had some inexplicable use for it. Somehow, it was only now, in this stripped down state, that Alecia recognized the woman as the person she had known in her original timeline as Jane Jones-Miller. Alecia was overcome with horror at the realization that made her stomach turn. She had to focus her mental energy on preventing herself from vomiting for several minutes, struggling through emotional tears. Though upset, she reminded herself that there was nothing else that she could do for her, and she did not want to be around to see how the impoverished citizens of Los Angeles would gather the rest of her. She needed to focus on her goal and find Dale, in the hopes of leaving this hellscape as soon as possible.

As she began to brainstorm strategies on how to go about finding this version of Dale, a familiar silhouette tugged at her peripheral vision. Alecia cautiously crept against the wall of the home, toward the light of a campfire in the quickly dimming evening light.

Alecia crept past the once decorative cobblestones and unmowed grass, her skepticism at her dumb luck gave way to certainty. There, by the fire was the familiar frame of Dale, albeit a little skinnier and with much longer hair, but it was him, slouched in a lawn chair. Several other bedraggled looking people sat in their own chairs in a haphazard circle around the small tire-rim fire pit. As Alecia's visage slowly formed in the fire light, out from the shadows of closely packed tents, she was faced with another heart-wrenching shock. Dale was filling a syringe from a freshly heated spoon, he rested the spoon gingerly and the chair's armrest, and with a swift motion, wrapped a thick rubber band around his left arm and quickly pumped his fist, to raise the veins.

"Stop!" Alecia shouted, lunging toward Dale in wide-eyed panic. The scraggly form of Dale barely reacted, other than a sideways glance and a scoff, "Yeah, right." "Why, Dale? Why are you doing this to yourself?" Alecia pleaded, her voice filled with pain and concern for the man, who in this world, barely knew her.

Dale shot her a venomous look, his eyes filled with self-loathing. "Why do you even care, *Officer Hernandez*? I'm just a worthless loser. We dated for what, five months in high school, and then you said you needed to focus on your goals, remember? Why the concern now? You're acting like we have some other connection, but we don't."

The other members of the campfire huddle had quickly and quietly melted into the shadows between the tents, not wanting to harsh their buzz with the commotion that had erupted. Self-preservation instincts told them it was best to put distance between themselves and anyone who had been apparently identified as a cop.

Alecia's heart shattered at Dale's words, the reality of her actions hitting her like a ton of bricks. She had lost the man she loved, and there was no way to fix what she had done.

"What do you want Alecia? Are you looking to make a bust? You wanna shake me down?" Dale's face was skeptical and accusatory. "You don't need this!" Alecia gestured to the squallor around her. "You're smart...you can have such a better life..." "Sure, and I'm sure you've got something for me that is going to help make that better life, right?"

"No, listen, I care about you..." "Yeah, right!" Dale interjected. "You're just another cop looking to line your pockets in the slums." Dale gestured toward the needle in his hand. "This! This is the only thing in my life that I've ever been able to count on." "NO, you can count on me! I..." "Fuck sake!" Dale interrupted. "Get it through your head lady! Not interested, leave me alone."

Defeated and sinking into silence, Alecia shrank away from her angry ex-lover. It was her turn to meld into the shadows of the tent city before he had a chance to see the silent tears running down Alecia's face.

Moments later, Alecia finished wiping away the tears and tried to compose herself, before some opportunistic stranger noticed. As she strode toward her hover-car, she recognized the familiar form of the man in the trenchcoat who'd sold her the Narcan canister. He was flanked by several other men, all as bedraggled looking as the rest of the denizens of this neighborhood. Alecia's anxiety rose, quickly surpassed by her anger at the memory of how this man had contributed to her failure to save someone that she had known as a friend in another life.

"Hey, Officer," the man greeted her, sounding more friendly than his sneering visage suggested. "I'm not buying anything else, sorry".

Alecia moved toward her car door, halting when the long trench coat moved to block her. "We ain't interested in sellin', *Officer*, we thought you'd be interested in makin' a donation." "Whatever it is, I'm not. Get out of my way." Alecia glared back firmly. The trenchcoat lifted his open hand in a "slow-down" gesture. "Now just wait," the man looked over his shoulder and gave a cocky grin to his cronies, then continued. "We been talkin' about why on earth a copper wouldn't have taken all the stuff off that dead lady when they had the chance, and we thought that maybe...well you must've thought...you weren't tough enough to keep it." Alecia looked around silently, eyeing up the men that were slowly moving in while their representative spoke. "And if that's the case, well we thought maybe a few big, strong guys like us, we could take care of this car for you, say, if you felt like walkin' home tonight, and you can tell your bosses that you donated it to the less fortunate." The man snickered and exchanged confident glances to his comrades. "We'll make sure every nut and bolt that comes out of this thing goes toward "community improvement". The man in the trench coat chuckled with that, which was echoed by the men slowly forming a circle around Alecia and her car.

The trenchcoated man's face burst in a stream of blood, mid-chuckle, as Alecia's elbow turned his nose into a bloody pulp in one shot, emitting a loud "crunch" noise. Before any of the homeless could register what was happening, Alecia's hand gripped the ring of scraggly, long black hair that rimmed the man's head and slammed his face hard into the side of her armored car. The man let out a groan as she released him, falling unconscious on the ground. Alecia looked up, waiting for hostilities to advance from the other men that were surrounding her, but they were already scrambling to get away from the woman that they'd clearly underestimated. "Fuck OFF!" Alecia screamed to the fleeing men before tapping a panel on the car that triggered the door to open.

As the car rose from the filthy street and into the air, Alecia broke into heavy sobs, filled with guilt and remorse over the horrors of the world she'd created. The dashboard beeped when the car had risen to the proper elevation, signaling that the driver needed to take control or input a destination.

Unbeknownst to Alecia, this version of Dale's mind was slipping into a state of euphoria that it would never return from. His body slowly relaxed in his chair as he absent mindedly dropped his empty heroin needle to the ground. His eyes closed for the last time, and in moments, his body would be wildly convulsing.

Through her tears Alecia had a realization. There was only one way to fix this. Still shaking through sobs, Alecia feebly reached forward and punched the button that told the car to return to its home docking station of Project Magenta.

The car parked itself in its rooftop home as Alecia worked to dry her eyes and compose herself. She exuded the image of a serious, no-nonsense Time Officer as she swiped through the rooftop security gate and strode with purpose toward the Time Officer locker room. Her military status, combined with alpha clearance ensured that her off-duty presence would not set off the same alarms that had triggered when she'd stormed the compound as a civilian mechanic, but the security team and the time lab would be given a notification of her unscheduled presence.

In a few swift motions Alecia quickly donned the padded time jump suit from her locker. To no great surprise, she was greeted by Gail, known for working long past her scheduled hours, usually too engrossed reviewing time data to watch the clock. Gail was hovering nervously in front of the entrance to the Time Lab as Alecia strode across the locker room. "What happened, Officer Hernandez?" Dr. Agu asked in a friendly, familiar tone. "You forget your sunglasses in your locker again?"

Alecia was unfazed by the friendly greeting, determined to undo what she had done to the entire world by trying to save the love of her life. "No Gail, listen," Alecia surprised her friend with her serious tone. "There's too much to explain, but I need to jump and it needs to be now."

Dr. Agu stammered in surprise at the nonchalant suggestion that they commit what was considered treason, since the advent of time technology became public. "Officer...Alecia," Gail's sudden panic caused her to appeal to their friendship, "we can't do that..." "Gail," Alecia responded, using the same trick the doctor had pulled back on her, "listen, something went wrong, I went back and something I did changed the present...things are not the way they are supposed to be!" "Officer Hernandez, " Gail said firmly, "If that's true, there is a process that we need to follow. We need to record your statement and review it with the time director to determine what, if anything, has been negatively altered and how to correct it." "There's no time for that Gail." Alecia said sternly. "I'm jumping now, whether you help me or not."

Alecia used some of the military bravado she'd learned in this timeline and pushed past the doctor and into the time lab. "That cannot happen." Gail said, grabbing her friend's shoulder is desperation. Alecia turned and looked at the hand on her shoulder and then into the thick glasses of her supervisor, "Do you really want to fight me, Gail?"

The doctor's grip nervously loosened as Alecia strode toward the Time Well platform. Gail, redirected the hand that had been on Alecia's shoulder moments before to a large red, wall-mounted plunger, triggering a security alarm. Alecia ignored the alarms, she knew that security would be there soon and she didn't have time for distractions.

She quickly tapped the familiar screens and buttons that brought the control console to life before firing up the glowing energy emitters.

Rippling pink energy began to spread out, filling the open mouth of the pit.

Alecia's gaze fell onto a panel that was unfamiliar to her. From her understanding of the data on the screen, it seemed that this timeline had figured out how to divert some of the temporal energy, allowing for a more targeted time jump. She had a brief moment of hesitation before tapping some info into the screen that she hoped would work to get her closer to her desired destination in the past.

Security guards entered the room, shouting orders to back away from the panel. Alecia refused to acknowledge them, but she did take a moment to glance at her concerned friend. Dr. Agu was framed by security guards as she pleaded, "Alecia, why are you doing this?" Alecia returned a serious expression, "Hopefully, you'll never need to know ", then dropped into the pit.

Chapter 7

Alecia awoke to a familiar yet disorienting location. She was in her own body, but the world around her had changed once more. She recognized her college dorm room. "Thank God, it must have worked." she muttered to herself, relieved that the data she had punched into the machine before jumping must have gotten her to, or at least close, to where she wanted to be. Alecia had had to make a split second decision before she'd made the jump. She'd decided it was too risky to go back and try to stop things, but she could find Dale in college, repair their relationship, and fix the negative trajectory that the previous version of Dale had taken into squalor. Alecia thought of the memory where she'd broken up with him, she remembered the hurt on his face, and her own heart hurt in response. Alecia's heart ached at the thought of their separation. The love she felt for Dale had never faded, even in this altered reality.

Alecia pulled back the faded pink sheets that had come to the dorm with her when she'd moved out of her suburban family home. Her roommate, Kasandra, was already dressed, putting the final couple of bobbie pins in her hair needed to keep it up. Alecia, opened her small armoire on the opposite wall, stripped off her night clothes, and was dressed and putting on her running shoes before Kasandra had even finished a final check of her hair in her desk mirror. "We're getting together with Lizzy and john and some others for brunch..." "Don't care, things to do." Alecia blurted as she went out the door, leaving her roommate confused by her abrupt rebuttal of brunch.

The UC Berkeley campus sprawled before her, a futuristic marvel of architecture and technology. It was vast and bustling with students, but Alecia was determined to locate the one person who mattered most to her.

Alecia hurriedly walked over to the student lounge and arcade. After her second thorough look around she'd determined that Dale was not there. Soon the same could be said of the library, and the rooftop smoking area. Alecia's stomach grumbled. "I guess the food court is as good a place to look as any." Alecia thought to herself.

A short time later, she was deep in thought, as she took a seat in a private corner with her turkey and avocado burger and fries. She'd forgotten how much she loved the food here. Alecia savored the flavor of the pretzel bun combined with the baja sauce, and slices of fresh avocado, atop a thick, perfectly grilled turkey patty. Her culinary delight eventually had to give way to the problem of how to find Dale somewhere on this enormous school campus. She was lost in thought, puzzling about what her next steps should be while munching one fry at a time, failing completely to notice classmates and acquaintances who had seen her and mumbled to each other about what was "up with Alecia today?"

In a rush of excitement, Alecia shoveled her last few fries into her mouth as she made a realization. She'd been thinking about the Dale she knew, but not as a Time Mechanics student. Sure, Mechanic students liked food too, but where did they go when they wanted to eat without spending any money? The school's large, public produce greenhouse. Alecia quickly returned her tray to the rack and walked briskly out of the cafeteria, oblivious to any other students still watching as she left, including one Kevin Kilroy.

The greenhouse was a huge, open public space. Beautiful, lush, fruit bearing trees were everywhere. Mangoes, bananas, oranges, apples, Avocados and various berries were easily at hand, a smorgasbord for those who were hungry, but didn't have or want to spend money on food. Large open pathways of crushed white stone separated different patches of plants. The walkways were populated with staff and students browsing for their next treat, or just enjoying the beauty of the place. Horticulture students busied themselves, checking the plants for any signs of needing more water, or needing a branch or two trimmed here or there. The 40 foot high glass walls and ceiling allowed ample room for the trees to grow, reaching high toward the sun, while the air circulation system kept the 20 acre greenhouse the perfect temperature, temperately warm for the plants, but not allowing it to reach scorching, oppressive temperatures that would hamper human enjoyment.

In just under five minutes, Alecia had explored enough to hone in on the sound of loud voices, laughing and releasing a plume of vape smoke. "Ah, there are the mechanics!" she thought to herself as she approached a group of 5 students congregating around, some sitting, some standing, some sitting on a brown picnic table that was parked in the shade of a cherry tree.

As she approached closer and her fellow students came into focus, she was a little dismayed to see that none of them was Dale. She'd come this far, there seemed little option but to continue her course of action. Besides, some of the students had noticed her approaching, giving her puzzled expressions as they slid their vape sticks back into the chest pockets of their coveralls.

"Hey, you guys are time mechanic students, right?" Alecia asked awkwardly, a little nervous given her experience with time travel so far. Somehow she felt like she wore the details of her crimes on her that anyone could read as soon as they looked at her. "Yep, we sure are!" a young man responded, still puffing on his vape.

"Awesome!" Alecia blurted, "So do any of you guys know Dale? Dale Yoshawa?"

"You're a friend of Dale's are you?" A young, coverall clad woman said with a bit of a catty tone. "Yes." Alecia replied timidly, unsure if this student was also a potential lover of Dale's in this timeline.

The first student who spoke dismissed his fellow student's accusational tone with a chuckle. "Well it looks like Dale has been holding out on us," he grinned. "I'm guessing you're in a different program?" Alecia simply nodded. "Well, you're not likely to find him anywhere on campus right now," the helpful student continued, "He's gone to the beach with some of our classmates. We finished our midterms this morning so everyone is looking to unwind. Our dorm is going to have a rager tonight."

A glimmer of hope, so this plan of action wasn't entirely wasted.

"What dorm would that be?" Alecia asked, suppressing her excitement at a potential lead. The other students looked around at each other, grinning at the question. "Most of us are in building "C", the kid who seemed to be their designated speaker offered, finally. At least that was the same as what Alecia remembered in her original timeline.

"Thanks." Alecia said as she turned away. "See you there, kitten." The jealous woman in overalls said in a sarcastic tone. Alecia didn't have time to start drama with someone that she told herself was probably perfectly nice in a different situation. She simply looked over her shoulder and gave a grin in response, instead of a fuck you, before walking away. The curious mechanic students watched her walk away, some with looks of jealousy, others of appreciation, commenting to each other under their breath.

As Alecia worked her way back toward the greenhouse entrance that she'd come in, she saw Kevin Kilroy, hovering around the entrance, pacing a little and watching Alecia with a scowl. As she walked past, hoping to ignore him, Kevin approached. "Slumming it with the gear heads now?" Kevin asked, accusatory. "None of your goddamn business, Kevin." Alecia put a sharp emphasis on his name at the end, implying an unspoken "fuck you".

"I don't get why you can't see potential right in front of you." Kevin pressed forward, entering Alecia's personal space. She rolled her eyes and glared directly into his, "Kevin, I do not have time for your shit today!" She responded. Kevin reached out, grabbing her forearm firmly. "We could be great together Alecia!" Kevin implored. Alecia angrily pulled her arm free of Kevin's grip, "No!". She had said it loud enough for bystanders, who started looking at the scene unfolding. Kevin scrambled after her, once again taking a firm hold of her forearm,

Alecia quickly broke the hold, grabbing his fingers and crushing them painfully before planting a knee, hard into his balls. "AAA! FUCK!" Kevin screamed, slumping to the ground in agony. Alecia continued walking as startled witnesses watched Kevin writhing on the ground. Some laughed, some clapped.

Now, with a potential timeline in mind, Alecia unhurriedly made her way back to her dorm. She found the weed that she expected in her armoire, rolled a couple of joints and then made her way to the student courtyard that rested between a number of large dorm buildings. She chose a nice bench, shaded by a walnut tree, where she could keep an eye on the entrance of "C" building. Alecia kicked her feet up, settled in and lit a joint.

Several hours later, the sky was dimming, casting long shadows across the campus courtyard in the early evening light. Half bleary from her marijuana, Alecia noticed a form that she thought looked familiar from across the courtyard, sauntering toward the dorm building that she'd been watching. Quickly closing some of the distance, by the time she'd crossed half of the courtyard, she'd mentally confirmed it was Dale.

Students were already milling about, preparing to unwind after months of study and practice. Some were getting an early start on drinking. Others milled about chatting, smoking vapes or joints of their own. "Dale!" Alecia called out to his turned back from about 20 feet away, worried that his quick pace would take him into the building and out of view before she could catch him. Dale paused and turned, a look of surprise quickly occupied his face. "Alecia?" he intoned with surprise. "Yes," she said, suddenly tongue tied as to what her plan had been from this point.

Alecia had noticed some of the mechanics she'd seen in the greenhouse, including 'Ms. Jealous' gathered nearby. She had been watching Alecia approaching Dale intently. Before she could begin explaining to Dale why the girl that had broken his heart was now calling out to him outside his dorm, she wanted to mitigate any unintended consequences or hostilities caused by her time travels. She looked sternly back at the catty mechanic. "Are we going to have a problem here?" Alecia asked her. "Nope," the potential rival responded without hesitation through a chuckle, "I saw how you handled that asshole in the greenhouse. You go get yours girl!" Some of the other students shared in the laughs while nursing drinks.

As Alecia's gaze returned to Dale, he gave her a puzzled look. "I'll explain later." Alecia said before Dale could form a question out loud. "Okay, what's up Alecia?" Dale asked, skeptical that this woman who had dumped him and walked out of his life a couple of years before was now standing outside of his residence, looking for him.

After a brief pause, Alecia looked deeply into Dale's eyes and said "I love you."

"I'm so sorry I hurt you," she continued, "I was wrong. I was afraid that a relationship would make me sacrifice my goals." Alecia thought of the life that she and Dale had in the original timeline and the sorrow of losing him. She slumped to her knees, oblivious to the onlookers now, pleading "I can't express how much I miss you every day...how your absence causes a black hole inside of me that grows every day...". Alecia's desperate rambling was interrupted by Dale, reaching out and holding her hands, then helping her to her feet. Dale looked into her eyes and said "You never have to beg me, just to be who you are." then kissed her. Alecia savored every moment of that kiss, as if she could absorb something from Dale's essence that was filling that empty feeling she'd been talking about. Cheers and cat calls erupted from the students watching nearby. Alecia smiled at her new supporters and kissed Dale again.

After a couple of drinks to be social, the pair retreated to Dale's dorm room. His dorm mate was partying somewhere else. Away from prying eyes the pair did some greatly needed reconnecting. They caught up, talking about what had happened in their lives in the last two years or so, Alecia being very careful not to say anything that let on that she was anything more than a college student, certainly not a time traveler. Alecia continued to make the apologies that she felt were necessary. Dale was gracious and made apologies for what he perceived were his own failings. Dale conceded that he had been torn up by the end of his relationship with Alecia, and that he'd equally felt something missing in his life since their relationship had ended. He admitted to thinking about her a lot. They eventually fell into comfortable topics, like family and goals for the future. By 2am, it was apparent that Dale's dorm mate had chosen to crash somewhere else that night. Alecia ached for his touch. She kissed him deeply, then took a few steps back, giving him a full view as she stripped.

The pair made mad, passionate love. Hands and mouths explored each other, releasing soft moans of pleasure from the dorm room. It was a culmination of years of longing and heartache, and it felt like coming home.

Exhausted and emotionally spent, they shared a post love-making joint that Alecia had been saving, careful to blow as much of the smoke out of the small dorm room window as possible. Naked as the day they were born, they fell asleep in each other's arms, their love rekindled in this new timeline where they had a chance to be together once more.

Chapter 8

Alecia tumbled out of the bottom of the Time Well, landing on the airbag below. As she caught her breath and started to get up, she noticed she was still wearing the time jumpsuit, not identical to the one she'd been wearing before the jump, the padding was slightly different, more angular. Alecia quickly took mental note of the fact that she was still dressed as a Time Officer, but the change in design clearly meant that she had caused some kind of change in the present timeline, and she couldn't help but feel a sense of unease.

Climbing up the ladder, she was met by an unfamiliar face in a lab coat. Alecia's breath caught in her throat as new memories began to integrate from this timeline. The chubby, smiling man at the top of the ladder was Dr. Matheson. In this reality, a new Time Force rule meant automatic retirement at 60 years of age. Alecia felt a pang of remorse, realizing that Dr. Agu had been long forced into retirement, meaning that many of the events that had built a bond of friendship between the two women had never happened. She was already starting to worry about what crazy changes her actions had made to the timeline now. Her heart sank at the realization that her actions in the past had far-reaching consequences on the people she cared about. She tried to gather her thoughts as she looked around, taking in the unfamiliar surroundings without showing any outward reactions that would make the scientists in the time lab suspicious.

Alecia gave a pensive look over her shoulder. Dale was there, still alive and well, hovering by the entrance to the time lab from the engine room in a pair of mechanics coveralls. She gave him a wink. Her mind was overcome with new memories and minute changes of choice that formed her new present. What mattered was that Dale was alive. They were a couple, but not married in this new timeline. Seeing him brought a mix of relief and guilt, knowing that her actions had shaped his life in unexpected ways.

"We'll have to get over to the Time Director briefing right away, while you still have the mission details in mind." Dr. Matheson informed her, breaking the mental rollercoaster that had been running through her head. "The mics in the pit seemed to have not caught much, if any audio data, so you'll need to be very detailed with the director."

The debrief room was still the small, dark box that Alecia hadn't been impressed with in the last timeline. The director hadn't shown up yet, leaving Alecia and Dr. Matheson to occupy the spots that she and Dr. Agu had sat in during her previous encounter with the Time Director. Of course that event had been erased, so Alecia was the only one who remembered it.

A side-door to the room, which entered from the Time Director's private office clicked open and a figure quickly strode into the room and occupied the chair behind the desk. Alecia's voice caught in her throat, her surprise showing on her face, betraying the calm exterior that she'd been trying to maintain through this whole time travel experience. No one who was aware of the ordeal she'd been through already would have blamed her. There, sitting in the chair of the Time Director, was Kevin Kilroy.

New memories were merging into Alecia's memory, recalling the stratospheric rise of Kevin Kilroy through the ranks of the Time Force. "How was your jump, Officer Hernandez?" Kevin smiled at Alecia from across the table. Somehow, even this pleasantry from Kilroy seemed laced with innuendo. Alecia took a deep breath and focused, recentering herself and keeping a calm demeanor, all the while thinking that she needed to satisfy the questions that would be asked, without doing anything that could divulge the time altering secrets that she was keeping. "Pretty standard." Alecia replied flatly.

Kilroy lofted a transparent tablet device in one hand, its screen displaying a series of charts and graphs. "It looks like there was a spike of chronal radiation on your descent. Did something go wrong with the objective?" "No, not at all." Alecia lied. Her own memory had filled in that she was supposed to give a young scientist a nudge toward a time formula that he would crack, leading to further advancements in the Time Force technology. Alecia absolutely had not performed the objective, but she played along. "Strange, we didn't see the progress in the objectives that we'd hope for, but a spike like that usually means that *something* happened." "Nothing more than the mission that I was assigned." Alecia kept up her flat tone. If she was going to have to lie to someone's face, there was no better choice than Kevin Kilroy. "What about secondary objectives? Did you do something to move the needle on any of our other overall goals?" Alecia searched new memories nervously, fumbling to come up with a response, ultimately going with "No, just the one...the primary objective. I...didn't have time to focus on much else." Kilroy paused, looking at Alecia silently and thoughtfully for a moment, then turned his attention to the doctor while handing him the device in his hand. "Take this and look over it. Do a diagnostic and see where we need to recalibrate the machines." "Yes, sir." the doctor responded obediently.

The debriefing was tense, and Alecia felt a growing sense of dread as Kilroy questioned her. She had to be careful with her words, fearing that any slip-up could reveal her secret. Kilroy seemed to relish his newfound power and authority, making the situation even more uncomfortable.

After a series of technical questions back and forth between Dr. Matheson and the Time Director, Kilroy seemed satisfied. "That will be all Doctor, you're dismissed. Officer Hernandez, and I still have some matters to discuss." "Great!" Alecia thought to herself sarcastically. As if being in the dark room answering to Kilroy wasn't bad enough, now she'd have to be alone with him in this cramped box.

After Matheson left the room, Kilroy looked at Alecia with a smirk. "You sure you didn't change anything else." "No sir." Alecia nearly choked on the words with mock surprise. "Come on, you didn't veer off the objective at all? You didn't sneak a quickie with a professor that you had a crush on or leave yourself a note." "No, sir." Alecia had regained her flat tone, now tinged with an edge of anger. "Oh, come on, Alecia, relax! We're old friends, aren't we? I know we're not supposed to, but no one's going to blame you if you tried to make things a little easier for yourself while making the world better too." "No sir, nothing like that." Alecia responded, irritation becoming evident. "Ok, ok." Kilroy chuckled.

To Alecia's surprise Kilroy stood, walking around the narrow passage between the desk and the dark walls, coming to sit casually on the corner of his desk, nearest to Alecia. "I have been dying for us to get some private time alone like this." All pretense of professionalism had melted away as Kilroy's face took on a lecherous sneer of approval, looking Alecia up and down. "That doesn't sound like official Time Force business." Alecia intoned flatly, unimpressed and concluding with an unfriendly glare at the Time Director. "How can you still be hung up on that mechanic?" Kilroy asked in exasperation. "How can you be happy spending so much time with someone that is so far beneath you?" Alecia had no intention of explaining herself or her love life to Kilroy, of all people. "I don't believe this line of questioning is considered appropriate according to standard harassment regulations..." "Okay, okay" Kilroy interrupted, holding up his hands in mock self-defense. "I thought that we could have a personal moment, but I see that you're as dedicated to doing things by the book as ever. You may go now, Officer."

"Thank you, *sir*." Alecia made no attempt to hide her contempt for the man that was now her boss. Making the word "sir" sound like a venomous insult. She rose from her seat and marched heavily for the door that would lead her out of this godforsaken room. Before she could reach for the handle that would allow her escape, Kilroy surged forward, grabbing her arms and pressing his body into hers, slamming her hard into the wall. "Kevin, what are you doing?" Alecia stammered angrily, repulsed to have a man she had nothing but disdain for so close and pressed against her body. Kilroy held her in place as she struggled, freeing one of his hands long enough to pull up his left sleeve, revealing a series of tally marks tattooed on his forearm, groups of 4 lines, crossed through with a fifth. Kilroy pressed his arm against the wall close to Alecia's angry face so that she could see it. "See this, huh?" Kilroy spat angrily. "There's a mark here for every female Time Force employee that I've had my cock inside. You think you're better than them? I've even been saving a special spot just for you. Whether it's today or tomorrow, you're going to beg me to take your place, even if I have to make you." spittle sprayed from Kilroy's mouth as he got worked up, losing his composure.

In response Alecia freed an arm from his grip and in a quick, sharp motion, planted her elbow firmly into the bridge of his nose with a crunch, spraying blood across his face. Unable to contain her rage any longer, Alecia gripped Kilroy's long hair firmly. "You sick, twisted bastard," she managed to say, before slamming his head into the top of his desk. Alecia leaned in closely, so that the startled senior commander could hear her. "You're not fit to lead anyone, let alone the Time Force." she spat, her voice trembling with fury.

Alecia shoved a groaning Kevin Kilroy to the floor, composed herself, putting on a fake veneer of pleasantness, and walked out of the room as if nothing happened.

"Shit," Alecia thought to herself as she walked calmly toward the time lab. "How the hell are my actions changing things so drastically? I have to fix this. I've completely fucked things up..."

"Arrest Officer Hernandez immediately! For assaulting the Time Director..." Kevin's voice screamed from the doorway down the hall behind her, his face and uniform covered in the blood that was still flowing from the explosion in the middle of his face that used to be his nose. The fact that security and other staff that had just been going about doing their jobs as usual were too startled by the sight of their bloodied boss and his screaming to react quickly worked to Alecia's advantage. She cleared the distance to the Time Well in seconds. Onlookers had no time to make the necessary mental computations to realize what she was doing. In a moment of bravery, Dr. Matheson stepped forward, attempting to block Alecia's access to the Time Well. "What are you doing?" Matheson asked, attempting to exude a tough demeanor and hide his nervousness. He was not very successful. Alecia returned a wordless cold stare that spoke volumes. Matheson sheepishly raised his hands and stepped out of the way.

Alecia's hands scrambled over the console panels feverishly as Security and other surprised staff approached the Time Well. She looked up to see a confused Dale in the entrance from the Engine Room. "I'm sorry, I have to fix this!" she shouted to her lover in the distance, then tossed herself into the pit, to the wide-eyed astonishment of her fellow lab workers.

Chapter 9

Alecia jolted awake in her teenage body, feeling disoriented by the sudden change in her surroundings. She glanced around her room, the posters of old musicians and bands on the walls, and the familiar feeling of her old bed. She'd been transported back to her teenage body, her hair was long and blonde, with streaks of neon pink and blue.

In a rush of panic, she scrambled out of bed, realizing that it was a school day, and she'd have to keep up appearances as usual, unless she felt like stretching her acting muscles and feigning illness at the last minute to get out of school. After a moment, she ruled out the thought of staying home. Thinking that if she had gone to school originally, staying home would be too much of a change, and she was just about fed up with the altered timelines she'd already encountered. No, it would be safest to go to school. She hurriedly got dressed, throwing on a gray tank top and pink leggings, with a burgundy hoodie tied around her waist. The memories of her high school routine flooding back. It was a surreal experience, and she couldn't help but feel a strange mix of nostalgia and apprehension. She grabbed her skateboard from the place it slept, leaned against the wall just inside of her bedroom door, and headed downstairs.

Downstairs, she found her father in the kitchen, sipping coffee and reading the newspaper. He looked up and smiled as she entered, not noticing how much Alecia was still brewing with turmoil, from a mind filled with memories of multiple lives. "Morning, sweetie. You're up early today."

Alecia managed a weak smile in return. "Yeah, Dad, just trying to get a head start on the day."

After a quick breakfast, she skated to the bus stop. The yellow school bus arrived, filled with suburban California kids, including Dale. Alecia tried to stay calm as she made her way to her seat, smiling at Dale as she passed, who returned the smile in kind. His eyes shone through a tousle of thin, tightly wound dreadlocks. Alecia's smile was widened by the fact that she'd forgotten about the time when Dale had long hair, and how much photos of the time would embarrass him in the future. She didn't care, she still thought it looked good on him, for a younger guy. They knew each other and had a friendly rapport, but in this timeline, they weren't dating, yet. She had bonded with him at a party where they both talked about how it felt to lose a parent. His father had passed six months before, and they'd Talked about it in a quiet corner, while everyone else was frolicking in the pool or making out. At least that was how it seemed to the young Dale, while in Alecia's mind, those emotional memories were many years old. She knew thanks to conversations they would have as a couple in the future that they were both crushing on each other at this time, but neither had made the move to become more than friends. Not yet. Alecia took her usual seat at the back of the bus, 2 seats behind Dale. All she had to do was nothing. Act normal, walk through a day in her teen life, and not change anything, unless a clear opportunity to undo some of the damage she'd seen in the future somehow presented itself. If she fell out of the Time Well and had to turn herself over to authorities in a world where Kilroy was in charge, she was going to be very pissed.

As the bus ride progressed, Alecia was distracted from her thoughts by motion in her peripheral vision. Looking closer, she couldn't help but notice Dale fiddling with a pack of cigarettes, passing one to a school mate in a seat across the aisle. Alecia thought of Dale's illness in the future and panic surged through her, she thought about the future where she had witnessed Dale's death. She couldn't stand the thought of him indulging in something that could harm him later.

Unable to contain herself, Alecia slipped in beside the kids who were in the seat directly in front of her, making a "shh" gesture with her fingers. A moment later she leaned over the back of Dale's seat and assertively took the cigarette pack from his hands. "Dale, you really shouldn't be smoking. They're not good for you," she teased, trying to pass off her attempt to save him as a teenage flirtation.

Dale looked at her in surprise, clearly caught off guard by being robbed of his smokes by the girl from the back of the bus. "Give those back!" he warned, his face flushing with embarrassment as the other kids on the bus started to watch. "I'm sorry, just trust me, you'll wind up better without them." Alecia grinned nervously at the awkward situation she'd put herself and her teenage crush in. Especially when she thought about how she wanted her past self to marry this crush in the future, again. "Alecia, come on." Dale said, getting annoyed. Dale's hand quickly shot forward to grab the cigarettes, but was too slow for Alecia's reflexes. She jerked back quickly, keeping the small pack just out of his reach. Murmurs and chuckles were starting to spread throughout the bus as more school-bound students took notice of the scene unfolding. Dale's face reddened, as barely audible murmurs of commentary from his peers watching in nearby seats began to reach his ears. "Gettin' bullied by a girl..." "...bitch in charge..." "...pussywhipped..." were just some of the comments making a young Dale feel like he was quickly losing face in front of his fellow students. His embarrassment quickly propelled to juvenile anger, cheeks hot with emotion. "Gimmie my smokes, BITCH!" Alecia was startled by the level of anger being unleashed toward her from someone she considered to be the love of her life.

Before she could even begin to start figuring out how to handle this situation, the bus lurched to a stop, jostling everyone off balance. "Sit the hell down back there you two!" the driver yelled, having noticed the confrontation thanks to a busload of whispering kids all facing the back of the bus. Alecia and Dale glared at each other briefly without speaking, before taking their seats.

Alecia's mind filled with dread at all of the possible ways that this new confrontation could alter the future for the worse, and how embarrassed she was by her poorly thought out actions. Upon arrival at school she had tried to hide her face and sneak away in shame, but when she saw the bus driver exit the bus and speak to Mrs. Alvarez, a gym teacher who was already not happy to be on bus monitor duty that week, she knew what it meant. She could feel Alvarez's icy glare through the back of her hoodie.

A few minutes later, she and Dale were sitting on opposite seats, outside of the principal's office, an empty few feet of walking space between them. Neither one wanted to talk to the other, so they both looked away from each other, scowling.

A few moments later they were seated side by side, still not looking at each other, in front of the principal of their suburban high school, Mr. Tobin. Tobin was a grandfatherly black man with thick glasses and a ring of gray hair around his otherwise bald head. "Now this is not the kind of thing I usually deal with from kids like you," The principal said, concern ruining his usual jovial appearance. "What happened?" "Nothing. Don't know what you're talking about." to his credit, the young Dale may have been a namecaller, but he wasn't a snitch. Alecia did her best to fake a totally puzzled look, as if she also had no idea what anyone was talking about. "Oh, is that what I'll see when I download the video from the bus cameras?" Alecia and Dale exchanged angry, nervous glances. "Please spare me. There's no way that bus driver wants to spend another minute with some of those kids on that bus than he has to. He certainly isn't going to stop the bus and stay on it any longer than he has to, unless it's necessary." Tobin fumed. "I heard that this was about cigarettes? I expected better from the both of you." Alecia and Dale were both looking at the ground now, immersed in the shame of their admonishment. "Gimme the cigarettes." Tobin stated firmly. Both students looked up, at each other, then away again nervously. "Come on, which one of ya has 'em?" The principal glared back and forth at the two students. A full minute of tense silence passed before Alecia quietly reached into the pocket of her denim backpack and tossed the cigarettes onto her principal's desk. When Dale saw the cigarettes slide across the principal's desk, he released a disappointed "Huff" and rolled his eyes.

"There, was that so hard?" Tobin asked with a mock grin. "Do I have your word that this is done?" the edge returned to his voice. The two students remained silent. They nervously looked at each other. "Do I?" "Yes," Alecia conceded. "Yeah." Dale nodded in agreement. Tobin stood and walked around his desk toward the students, "Now like I said, I've never had either one of you in my office for a disciplinary issue before, so I'm gonna let you go back to class."

"Thank you, sir." Alecia said, eager to get out of the awkward situation and get some privacy so that she could think about how she could salvage this day. Dale trailed behind her. Just as Alecia thought she'd be able to make a clean break without being embarrassed further, Tobin's voice came from his office door. "And I will be talking to both of your parents' about this before the end of the day." Both students let out a disappointed groan as they heard the news, somberly marching out of the larger main school office.

"I'm sorry." Alecia turned and said to Dale before he could escape in the other direction. In response Dale gave a silent tight-lipped expression with an eye roll that said, "yeah, thanks." in a sarcastic manner, before he turned away, picking up speed before he was any later for class. Alecia walked to first period Biology by muscle memory, her mind occupied with thoughts of all the ways this day had already gone wrong and how she could stop them from preventing future catastrophes. She didn't absorb a single thing said in class. 2nd period Programming was the same. By lunch, the whole school knew about what happened and kids that she didn't even know were giving her weird looks and whispering to each other. She wanted to hide in a corner and die.

She worried about how every step she took that day might be hurting Dale or someone else she knew. She felt like her mind would crack under the stress of knowledge. No wonder the Time Force had rules against abusing time travel for personal use. The extremeness of all the changes she'd experienced so far made no sense, so much so that she felt overwhelmed with trying to come up with a series of actions that would help her fix them.

After school, Alecia approached Dale where other students congregated to wait for the arrival of their bus. "Dale, I'm really sorry," she said. "I didn't mean for things to get out of hand like that." Dale gave a half-hearted smile, "My mom left work to come talk to the principal in person." Dale gestured with a nod toward the school. Just outside of the bus pick-up area, Dale's mom, legal briefcase in hand, was talking with Mr. Tobin. The kids stared in horror as they watched Tobin hand the pack of cigarettes to Dale's mother. She instantly recognized it as the pack she'd thought she'd lost before leaving for work this morning. She glared towards the two wide-eyed teens. Without breaking her stare, Mrs. Yoshawa stomped angrily to a nearby robotic trash receptacle and tossed them in before thanking the principal and moving toward them, eyes never leaving their target.

The teens both turned away from the gaze nervously. Dale's mother stormed up beside him, pausing momentarily to speak. "You're coming with me!" she said. "Since you can't be trusted to take the bus, I'll be driving you to and from school for a while, young man." Reina Yoshawa had already continued walking toward her car in the parking lot before finishing her sentence, expecting without question that her son would soon be following, if he knew what was good for him. "Great job, Hernandez." Dale said sarcastically, then turned and strode away, trying to catch up with his mother.

It was one, quiet, awkward bus ride home. Alecia spent most of it scrunched up in her seat deep in thought and trying not to be seen.

Alecia swiftly exited her school bus and strode swiftly into the repair garage that her father ran his business out of. She knew there was no point in trying to avoid her father, Principal Tobin had surely already spoken to him on the phone. Alecia dejectedly strode past her father without pausing to look as his hands turned a wrench on a hover bike sat atop a workbench. She somberly slumped into a tall chair behind the parts cluttered service counter and let her backpack slide to the floor, landing with a soft thud.

Brian Hernandez gave a sideways, speculative stare, he didn't lose any speed, tightening bolts without having to look. "So what happened?" the father said, an accusatory edge to his voice. "I hear you're stealing cigarettes from kids on the bus now?"

Alecia's emotions bubbled to the surface like a geyser, failing to prevent the tears that began to form. "No, it wasn't like that…" Alecia stammered. "I didn't mean to…that's not what was supposed to happen…" The big man with the ratchet had stopped his work, turning his full attention to his emotional daughter. "There's this kid I know from the bus…Dale…" Alecia wasn't sure how to continue this story. She was overwhelmed with the idea of just how much she had to edit out of her explanation. The whole thing about being from a future where she was married to Dale would not help her situation to share. She didn't want to risk waking up in a rubber room when she returned to her present.

"So, is this really about a boy?" Mr. Hernandez quipped, insightfully. Alecia hadn't been able to form the words to respond yet when the phone in the pocket of her father's coveralls rang. The big man slipped the small rectangular device out of his pocket and held it to his head. "Hernandez Auto Maintenance and Repair." Her father always used a happy tone with a smile when he answered during business hours. It charmed a lot of the regular clientele, because you could hear the smile in his voice. "Yes…" his tone changed, taking on an impression of serious interest with the voice on the other end of the phone, "Yes…I'm talking to her about it right now."

Alecia's stomach flipped. "Oh my god!" she mumbled, realizing that it was Dale's mother on the phone. Her cheeks flushed with new surges of embarrassment. Brian hung up the phone and returned it to his pocket. "This kid's mother is coming over to talk about what happened," stress bled into his voice. "You go inside and program the food machine for dinner. I'll be in after I close up, we can talk about this later."

Alecia did as she was told, slowly and dramatically sauntering into the house from an entrance at the back of the garage, dragging her denim backpack the whole way. Sitting in the kitchen to be tortured by her own thoughts in silence was too much and quickly became tiresome. Alecia went to the living room, nearest the garage, hovering and pacing in the hopes of catching any important sounds from her father's workspace. Mrs. Yoshawa, with Dale in tow, showed up just as Alecia's father was preparing to close up shop. She couldn't hear the words of the discussion clearly, just the murmur of familiar voices and half-words that she couldn't make out. She was much too emotional and deeply embarrassed to go out there and face them, listening from her hidden vantage point inside the doorway as she curled into a ball of anxiety and slow tears on the floor.

After the Yoshawa's left and Brian closed the shop, he entered his home through the back of his shop to find his daughter sitting on the floor, back to the wall, wiping tears in a sudden rush to compose herself. The big man rested a hand on her head and gave her hair a small tussle, "It's gonna be okay kid, we can talk about it after dinner."

Alecia shared an awkward meal with her father. Each picked at their food machine produced barbecue chicken silently, between small talk and careful questions about their day, avoiding the incident that still hung over Alecia like a storm cloud. After dinner, Alecia did her regular chore of clearing the dishes and setting the dish sanitizer. Her father had taken his usual after dinner position on the living room couch. Alecia was still a bundle of emotions that she couldn't keep restrained, feeling like she could break down into tears under the weight of all the knowledge in her head and memories of how distorted everything became each time she tried to fix it. She just wanted this day to be over, so that she could face whatever fresh new horror awaited in her present. She knew she wouldn't be able to talk without weeping. She just wanted to sneak up to her room quietly and go to bed. That was the plan, at least.

As she tiptoed towards the stairs to her room, just feet away from the steps, her father's voice called out from the living room beyond. "Hey honey, come here."

Alecia slowly inched into the doorway, head hung in shame, refusing to look at her father, tears in her eyes for all of the details that she couldn't tell him. She was pulled out of her shameful mire by her father's voice, she looked up through bleary eyes. "Wanna come watch a movie with me?" His voice was surprisingly upbeat as he fluffed a cushion on the couch next to him, indicating that Alecia should take a seat.

Alecia had forgotten how much she had loved cuddling up with her father on the couch and watching old movies together. "Sure," Alecia replied with a half-hearted grin as she closed the distance of the room and took a seat. Her fathers big hands played over the remote control in his hand. Cover images of hundreds of movies from all different eras flew by on the streaming menu of the wall sized screen in front of them, on the opposite side of the room. As he perused an unending list of options, Alecia's father spoke. "Like I said, it's gonna be okay." Alecia's eyes teared up, new waves of shame and self-doubt flooding her mind. "Mrs. Yoshawa is more pissed about her kid stealing her cigarettes than anything, but she doesn't think you and Dale should be hanging out, at least for the time being." Alecia released a heavy sob. "So this is a boy you like?" Brian asked insightfully. "Yes," Alecia managed to mutter through her tears. "Then why would you steal his cigarettes?" her father asked. Exasperated, Alecia blurted "I didn't mean to. I mean...I didn't want the cigarettes...I just wanted him not to smoke them." "So you wanted to be the hero?" Brian asked. Alecia nodded pathetically. "Honey, something you'll find out about boys your age, is that they don't always know what's good for them." "I had that problem myself when I first met your mother," the elder Hernandez chuckled. "She had to do a lot of work to get me to smarten up. I was hoping it would be a little longer before you had to learn the same lesson, but we play the hand we're dealt."

"I ruined everything, Dad! You don't even know how much I screwed up." Alecia blurted through tears and a mind flooded with memories that she couldn't share. Alecia's father wrapped a strong arm around his daughter's shoulders, squeezing her tightly. "It feels like that right now honey, but I promise, this will pass sooner than you think. Everything will be fine, and one day you'll have forgotten all about it."

Alecia was tired of thinking and being weighed down by the memories of her time traveling failures. She'd forgotten how much she had enjoyed being held close by her father, breathing in the smell of cologne and engine oil that seemed fused to his body. She decided there was no point in thinking or speaking further, and nuzzled in closer to her father, hoping to drown out the pressures of adulthood and enjoy an embrace that she'd been missing for years.

Her father had chosen V for Vendetta. Feeling a rush of excitement, her eyes were glued to the TV. She knew this movie was like a hundred years old or something, but she didn't care, it was one of her and her father's favorite movies to watch together. Alecia laid her head comfortably on her father's chest, interrupting the cinematic experience only twice, once to make popcorn and the other to chat briefly about some of her late mother's favorite old movies.

As the credits rolled, Brian Hernandez looked down at his daughter's head resting on his chest, realizing that she was already fast asleep.

Chapter 10

Alecia tumbled out of the Time Well once more, her jumpsuit altered again, but she was beginning to get used to the constant changes in her reality. This time, she was a Time Officer again. Her meddling with the past had continued to make unexpected changes to her present.

Alecia was pleased to see the smiling face of Gail Agu, back in her familiar lab coat, waiting at the top of the ladder. She looked pensively over her shoulder toward the engine room. No Dale. At least not that she could see. As new memories rose up to merge with her existing ones, Alecia realized that in this timeline, she did not know where Dale was. In spite of her father's reassurance, the cigarette incident had been the end of her and Dale's burgeoning romance in this timeline. Dale had avoided her, likely due to embarrassment, keeping their interactions limited to few words and awkward sightings in passing. In this reality, Alecia had settled for watching him from afar, hoping for a chance to smooth things over that never presented itself. After high school she'd completely lost track of him. Apparently this new timeline must have led Dale on a completely different career path. Alecia was sad to know that Gail and her other friends had never met him. It was going to make things very difficult if she ever had to talk to Gail about her time jumping.

Alecia sat through another debrief with Gail and the time director. Thankfully, Kevin Kilroy was back to being a Time Officer in this timeline, and another one of the board of Time Directors that she'd known, this time a dark haired woman in her late 50s, was Time Director.

Alecia once again, mentally tiptoed around saying anything that would tip her colleagues off to the fact that the timeline had been altered immensely. To those in the present, it hadn't yet been 24 hours since Alecia had made her first time jump to save Dale. To Alecia, it felt like several unyielding days of non-stop action. By some mystery of science, the Time Well had a rejuvenating effect. It wasn't that falling through the pink energy of the machine made you younger, but as detailed in many university course case studies, Time Officers often reported feeling as if they had more energy and felt more rested after passing through the field then they had before. It was like that tissue thin layer of waves somehow disassembled you when you entered and rebuilt you into the same form, with the same memories, but made of brand new atoms that hadn't experienced the lifetime of environmental and chemical stresses that the person had experienced beforehand. One of the Force's science missions was to study these effects. Time Officers bodies emitted less Radiation and the surface of their skin and cells of their bodies harbored much less potentially harmful bacteria than before they dropped into the well. The cause of this was still a mystery, with multiple scientific theories being explored.

Alecia was thankful for the well's rejuvenation as she bluffed her way through questions about her mission objective; to mention something in front of her schoolmate's parent that would trigger a thought, that would trigger a desirable action that would make the world of the future better. She feigned ignorance as to any explanation for the strange spikes in the chronal radiation charts, and Gail was again instructed to run diagnostics and recalibrate. Alecia was happy to march out of the debrief room with Gail after they were dismissed.

"Have a good night Officer Hernandez," Dr. Agu smiled happily, heading back toward the workstation that she herself was supposed to be done working at for the day, but knowing she would spend at least a couple more hours at before she left.

Alecia paused for a moment, as her lingering questions about the Dale of this timeline coalesced into a plan. "Actually, I'm going to take a note from your book," Gail's eyebrow raised inquisitively at Alecia's comment. "I...I need to do some more research...for this case." Alecia hoped that her clumsy words didn't somehow reveal her deep time wrecking secrets, "I'm going to head up to the archive." "Okay, well...have fun." Gail returned a friendly, surprised expression.

Alecia walked briskly to the Time Officer locker room, then quickly slipped out of her time jumpsuit and into her Officer's uniform. She was thankful that her speed had prevented the opportunity for anyone, especially Kevin Kilroy, to sexually harass her, or just generally fuck with her day.

The archive was a massive database library maintained by the Time Force. The huge stainless steel room was lit by an entire wall of large clear glass windows that allowed ample light with minimal electrical light fixtures. The other three walls were lined with the shiny metal sheeting. The room was four stories tall, marked out by numbers painted on the walls and the metal grating that passed for the floor and stairs needed to reach them, at each level. The metal grids ringed the room, allowing ample visuals of the many Time Officers on different levels, making use of this central repository of knowledge. Each level of the metal grating held a row of large blue file cabinets that held physical copies of important documents as a backup, in the unlikely case that something should cause a server failure. A pair of glass elevators on the opposite side of the room constantly zipped up and down. Moving Time Officers, and File Clerks with bundles of new hardcopies to be filed, about their business. Alecia took the stairs, slowly taking in her surroundings, noticing minor differences in familiar faces and totally new ones. She was searching the room for any sign of something or someone familiar. Maybe Dale was a File Clerk that she hadn't met yet in this timeline.

Alecia chose a workstation on the main floor that had a few empty stations around it. She knew that her job gave her all the authority she needed to do what she was doing, but she still felt the need for some privacy and to avoid prying eyes. She felt as if someone would look over her shoulder at her research and they would somehow know her whole timeline altering story and expose her on the spot. It was silly, deep down she knew that, but maintaining some stealthy behavior comforted her right now and kept her mind from wandering onto more depressing things. She leaned forward, allowing the retinal scanner on the top of the screen in front of her to examine her eye, then hum and flicker to life. There was no need for a login or password with a retinal scan, so Alecia was treated with a personal hello message and her preferred desktop design with search access to all of the information in the Time Force databases as well Infoweb service.

Alecia made the slow crawl to find out what happened to this Timeline's version of Dale. She was hopeful, that against all odds, she might be able to find him, meet, fall in love and not have to Time Jump again. Her guilt tied her stomach in knots. So far, this timeline seemed like it was the best of all of the one's she'd created. Sure, there were some imperfections, but this timeline had Gail and she hadn't been hit on by Kevin Kilroy yet, if she could find Dale, it just might be worth leaving things as they were.

This world's Dale didn't have the same criminal record as the one she'd met with a needle in his arm. Alecia decided to take that as a good sign. Changing her approach, she went with what she knew. Dale would have been a student of Lake Tahoe High around 2174, just like she was. There wasn't much to find. A couple of articles cross referenced him winning a silver medal in hurdles at a state-level track and field event. A few other Dale Yoshawa's of different ages and geographic locations. There was nothing to find about Dale after highschool.

Frustrated Alecia did a broad search of the name on the infoweb, scrolling through years worth of websites and info about other Dale Yoshawas. Just as she was about to give up hope that one of the most massive databases of info in the modern world was going to be another wrong path, she came across a series of articles from 2180. There was a cross reference link to an obituary. Alecia's frustration turned into trepidation. She carefully tapped the screen in front of her, as if she thought that if she tapped it too hard, it would make the information that she feared was waiting behind that click true.

Alecia's heart sank as she read the details, and matching pictures from a much happier time. This timeline's Dale Yoshawa, the one she knew, was dead. He'd taken a bottle of sleeping pills a year after completing high school. According to the article, it was an unexpected suicide. Alecia's heart sank. The Time Force rarely needed to be directly involved in straight forward death or murder investigations. Alecia accessed the civilian investigation database and pulled up the documents filed by investigating officers as well as the coroner's report. No note. No sign of drugs or emotional problems. Just dead from a bottle of pills one day. It didn't fit, it certainly didn't seem like the Dale she knew, but this wasn't the timeline she knew either. She had no idea how things could have changed in Dale's life since they were fifteen, and it would be next to pointless to reinvestigate the incident with the details at hand, from a cut and dried case nearly a decade old.

Alecia's heart sank. She stared down at the floor for several minutes, fretting about what to do and trying not to break down in tears. She thought, in her arrogance, that she could single-handedly change the world and rip her lover from the jaws of death. All she'd actually done was make things worse each time she tried to fix it. Now she'd managed, exactly how was still beyond her, to create a timeline where things were generally back to the way she had remembered them, but there was no Dale. There was no one to blame but herself. The thought crushed her.

Alecia quietly powered down the workstation and walked across the archive, toward the public washrooms. She looked down, avoiding eye contact the entire way, as if the stares of strangers would hold judgment, somehow knowing about the mess she'd made of the timeline. The walls of the women's room gleamed. Stainless steel walls and stall doors matched the look of Archive outside, with polished metal mirrors over a tasteful green marble tiled floor. Alecia was relieved that the cleaning bots had been through recently, and that there was no one currently using the facilities to witness her. She made her way to the farthest stall in the back corner of the narrow room and entered. Fighting now to suppress tears and ragged sobs, she pressed against the wall and slid down to the floor, wedged between a steel wall and the toilet. The moment that her body had come to rest on the floor, she released all of the heartache and remorse that had been building up since she'd embarked on her mission to change the past. Loud heaving sobs and painful wails flowed out of Alecia uncontrollably, mixed with a grief that she hadn't completely processed before she embarked on her personal mission. Alecia was mad at herself. She hated herself for ruining everything. She hadn't just failed to rescue Dale, she'd made life worse than the world she had started with every time she'd tried to make it better. She was never supposed to be a Time Officer, let alone experience time travel. Her irresponsible meddling had ruined everything. She should have listened to Gail, but it tore her up inside to think that there could be a better, proper timeline, without Dale. Her wails had reached such a volume that she hadn't heard someone else enter the ladies room. Between sobs, Alecia faintly registered the shuffle of feet. Her stomach flipped. Now she had to live with the embarrassment that someone had heard her emotional meltdown.

She glanced under the door and saw a pair of black Time Officer boots. Her mind slowly registered that the shoes she was staring at had not only stopped moving, but were standing a few feet away, facing the door of the stall that she occupied. Someone was watching her, or at least listening to her, just outside the stall. Her mind suddenly felt creeped out. She couldn't be certain from her vantage point, but the style and stance of the feet that she saw seemed distinctly male. Some guy was in the ladies room, enjoying a front row ticket to Alecia's mental breakdown. Alecia's mind was now pulled out of her pit of despair by curiosity, and she'd unconsciously subdued her sobs. After the brief moment of quiet, the mysterious watcher must have realized that something had changed or perhaps they'd been noticed. The mystery feet turned and quickly scrambled out of the washroom by the time Alecia had opened the stall door.

Alecia quickly wiped her face in a feeble attempt to hide the emotional torment she'd been experiencing and hustled out the washroom door. It was too late. Whoever it was had blended in with a room where most of the people were wearing the same uniform and going about their job of investigating and researching.

Exhausted with the events of the day and her raw emotions still boiling below the surface, Alecia decided that it was time to go home. She made one more attempt to wipe her face clear of tears and put on a well composed facade as she walked toward the elevator that would take her to the rooftop parking lot. During her journey upward, she had formulated enough clear thoughts that she'd decided it was okay to take a night and sleep on what her next moves would be. Tomorrow, she might risk talking to Gail about it. Since she was a Time Officer now, she had access to the Time Well, and could feasibly use it to try to fix the issues of this timeline under the guise of an assigned mission, without having to repeat the adrenaline ride of breaking in, as she had before. Alecia wasn't convinced if she should try to change anything or save Dale any more. Her heart was broken and she swallowed hard to fight back tears. She wasn't sure that she should ever be allowed to time travel again with how bad she kept screwing things up.

Alecia exited the elevator into the dimly lit bottom floor of the parking garage, usually reserved for vehicles that didn't fly, those had to us the tunnel that went down and out to the street, and Time Force vehicles that were not meant for daily use, such as S.W.A.T. and other heavy armored vehicles. The flying cars that saw daily use were stored in the 3 levels above. An open-faced lift was placed on the far end of the garage for people to travel between levels, but Alecia preferred the stairs, making her way across the lot and toward them. As she did, Alecia heard the distinct shuffle of feet behind her.

She slowly stopped and turned around to look. The sound had stopped and there was no one there. She turned back to her objective, the stairs, and took a couple more steps before she heard a rustling from the shadows. She paused and looked around again. She didn't want to be paranoid, but it seemed clear to her that someone was following her, watching from the shadows, just out of sight. She did not like that, and her mind began to race with panic. "Who the hell has a reason to follow me?" she thought.

In a split moment decision, Alecia bolted into the shadows on the opposite side of the garage from where the sounds of her potential assailant had come from. She slid behind one of the many load bearing concrete walls scattered throughout the parking lot that helped the building maintain its integrity. As much as she felt that she was unworthy of being a Time Officer, she had to admit, the training kept coming in handy. She slid along the wall, backtracking, slipping out from around the wall near the elevator she'd taken to get here. She'd be behind the mysterious figure that had been watching her, if they were still standing near where Alecia had been before she dove into the shadows.

Alecia crouched low, peeking around the wall that partially concealed her vantage point. She stared at the empty looking parking garage for tense seconds that felt like hours. Slowly, a dark form emerged. It was clearly a man in a Time Officer uniform, but the figure was too far away and too dimly lit to make out any other details from the silhouette. Alecia ducked back as the silent figure suddenly became animated, looking around as if confused. Alecia had clearly given her pursuer the slip, but it didn't give her many options for getting to her car. Alecia risked another peek, to see if she could gather any other insights from the silhouette, just in time to see him quickly dash over to the lift and hit the button that would take it and its passenger to the upper parking levels.

Was he still looking for Alecia, or had he given up and gone off to do his duty or head home? Alecia didn't like the idea of someone following her and she wanted to know why. No creepy stalker was going to follow her. In a moment of bravery she decided that she would think on this further after she'd safely made it to her car. She sprinted across the same distance she'd walked just moments before and bolted up the stairs, working her way to the top floor area where she knew her car would be. When she approached the final door at the top of the staircase that allowed access to the top parking level she slowed. She cautiously looked through the wire enforced window in the door at her police vehicle, still comfortably parked where the docking arm had placed it after her arrival.

In her peripheral vision she noticed motion. She ducked back before cautiously leaning forward to take another look. There, just beyond the daylight, in the shadowy corner of the parking level, was the same mysterious male silhouette. The once composed figure seemed to be fidgeting nervously. Pacing slightly as his gaze kept looking around for something, then back at a stationary position. It took a moment for Alecia to realize that her mystery stalker was standing in the shadows watching her armored police car. His movements likely reflected his frustration that he knew that he'd followed her in here, but now, she was not where she was expected. "How do they know where I'm parked?" Alecia thought. A cold shiver of anxiety ran down her body over realizing that she was indeed being pursued by another Time Officer in a clandestine way for some unknown reason. "Could they be suspicious of me?" Alecia thought, terrified that she was being pursued as a time criminal. "It doesn't make sense. How could it be that? How would anyone, other than me and a few easily dismissed radiation spikes, know how badly I've screwed the timeline?" Alecia's mind raced with dread and visions of potential incarceration.

As Alecia peered cautiously through the window of the metal door, her would-be assailant finally stepped into the evening light, aggravation causing him to drop his guard and forget the protection of the shadows. Her stomach did its tenth flip of the day when her eyes focused on the figure of Kevin Kilroy. "Great, just when I thought this might be the timeline where he wasn't a problem," Alecia thought. "Why is Kevin Kilroy following me?" She and Kevin were not assigned partners in this timeline, and as far as this world was concerned, Dale essentially didn't exist. There was no reason that Alecia could think of that she and Kevin would be connected or he would be following her.

A few minutes later, the dejected silhouette of Officer Kevin Kilroy sauntered over the lift he'd taken up and disappeared as it slowly lowered him back down. After a few seconds Alecia squeezed a handle, popping open the door that had served as her secluded vantage point. Alecia's eyes darted back and forth cautiously, worried that Kevin's disappearance could have been an elaborate ruse to trick her into showing herself, but there were no more trailing footfalls as Alecia quickly made her way to her vehicle.

Alecia hit the button that started the engine of the flying car, signaling the long, robotic docking arm to gingerly wrap its orange painted metal claws around the car. Once the programmed operation of the docking arm adjusted its claws from above to underneath the car and jockied it into a safe takeoff position, the claws slowly released in a smooth motion, allowing the car to gently rise upward and into the busy skies over Los Angeles.

As the car gently rose, Alecia's mind was now consumed with the strangeness she'd witnessed in the parking garage. "Why the Hell is Kevin Kilroy following me?" the thought nagged at her mind. All she had wanted to do was go home and sleep on her situation and regroup with a new plan in the morning. Now she wasn't sure she'd be able to. Alecia decided to use her car's access to the Infoweb to learn more about Kevin Kilroy in this new timeline. A quick skim of the files that came up revealed nothing outstanding or important. No smoking guns. In fact, it appeared that this Kevin had always kept his nose clean. No infractions, no disciplinary reviews, nothing to show he even held an extreme or contrary opinion. Either this version of Kevin was a boy scout, or he was very good at hiding his dirty laundry. Alecia guessed that it was the latter, based on the fact that he was secretly stalking women from the shadows of parking garages.

A new rush of endorphins told Alecia that she wasn't going to sleep any time soon. With no way to further her failed attempts at resurrecting Dale through time travel, figuring out why the hell Officer Kilroy was following her was the next best thing. If he could follow her, why couldn't she follow him? Turn about was fairplay, after all. Alecia punched the address listed in Kilroy's personnel profile into her car's navigation system with a tap of the screen. The car began to propel itself forward, slowly at first, then picking up speed until it was moving at 80km/h through the air over the city, barrelling toward the home of Kevin Kilroy.

Minutes later, Alecia's armored vehicle was slowly descending from the sky, hovering over rooftops of concrete and glass walled apartment buildings and offices. The address of Kilroy's home was a massive concrete building, a military barracks, the exterior of which was almost as cold and uninviting as the Project Magenta compound. Alecia took control of her car, guiding it to land on the roof of a building across the street, where she hoped she would be out of sight and go unnoticed. She took the standard issue field binoculars out of the car's glove box, watching junior Time Officers and military personnel coming in and out through the automated security gate.

The more she learned about this version of Kevin Kilroy, the more puzzling it became. Most Time Officers of his standing and experience would have had a family and purchased off-base housing, or at least moved into off-base military housing, like Alecia's condo. Most of the personnel who lived in these barracks buildings were trainees, or rookies who hadn't had the time or experience yet to think about settling down or engage in a serious personal life. "Why would Kevin choose to still be living here?" Alecia thought.

Much to her relief, Alecia didn't have to wait long for the subject of her interest to arrive. A blue dot and beep signaled to Alecia that the vehicle registered to Kevin, which she was able to track through her car's computers, was in the vicinity. Kevin's car descended from the clouds above California and gently jockied into position, waiting for the automated rooftop docking arm that would take hold and place it in the ideal space on the roof moments later. Kevin was home, but Alecia hoped that his actions, oblivious of her surveillance, would reveal something to explain the differences in this new timeline, and if it was worth keeping or if Alecia should push through the guilt and continue her mission to fix what she felt she'd he'd made worse. She knew it was a risk, but she hoped she hadn't rolled the dice just to stare at a concrete wall with narrow windows in it all night. She was slightly relieved when, 28 minutes later, Kevin emerged through the street-level security door. He looked like he'd freshened up, but was still wearing his black Time Officer uniform. Kevin in every timeline seemed to have a habit of wearing his uniform, even when he was off-duty. Had he showered and put his uniform back on, or did he have an extra one at home? Alecia knew that either answer was admittedly weird, she'd personally never brought a work uniform home, but weird wasn't the same as some kind of smoking gun.

As Kevin hit the sidewalk at a brisk pace, he passed a pair of young Time Officers as they approached the building, heading in for a night of poker and beer pong with the other rookies and trainees. The young officers beamed at Kevin stopping to say hi and chat. Kevin laughed along with them. He looked simultaneously more jovial and confident than she'd seen in any of the various versions of Kevin she'd met. "That's what it is!" Alecia thought to herself. "That's why he still lives in barracks as a senior officer. These guys look up to him. He loves the adoration and respect he gets." An experienced officer in the barracks when she was a trainee would have been considered a legend. His ego was soaking in all of the free respect and influence. Alecia felt slightly sickened that all those young officers thought this guy was a legend, when he was much more likely, a sociopath.

After a few moments Kevin and the rookies parted ways, Kevin continued padding at a brisk pace on foot, down the busy street.

Alecia hoped out of her car, deciding she'd have to leave it where it was and pursue on foot, one person being a lot easier to remain unnoticed than a massive, flying armored car. She ran quickly across the tar and gravel roof of the building she'd parked on, to the metal ladder that jutted just a few feet above the beige brick. Alecia quickly turned her body and hopped over the edge of the building. Bracing for speed control with the flats of her feet against the outer rails of the ladder and her hands loosely gripping the outside of the rails, she slid at a dizzying speed down several stories without using a single horizontal rung of the ladder as a handhold, like she'd been trained to in the military. She released the rail at the bottom, hopping down the final few feet with just enough time to spread her limbs and land on all fours, dispersing some of the shock of impact caused by her quick descent.

Alecia stood and quickly merged with the pedestrian traffic of Los Angeles. She strained to keep an eye on Officer Kilroy at a distance, anxious that she'd lost him several times, but each time her faith in continuing to move briskly through the tightly packed pedestrians paid off, with the oblivious Officer returning to view after a few moments in the shifting wall of bodies. Alecia finally slowed and ducked into a hookah cafe down the street when she saw the Officer hop into a local bar, a spring of excitement in his step. "Ugh. Fitting." Alecia thought. Alecia was already picturing how someone like Kevin, who relished special treatment, would behave in a local bar. When he showed up in uniform like this, he likely drank for free. If the other bar patrons didn't keep buying him rounds, the bartender would probably not charge him at the end of the night. Amazing how wearing a constant reminder that you can put people in jail gets a lot of them to kiss your ass like that, especially when you're wearing a military issued gun, taser and baton. Sure, some of the adoration is real, but some of them downright hate him and are just keeping up appearances in his presence. "That doesn't matter to him though," Alecia thought, "He'll soak up all the power and respect that the badge can give him, so he can go to bed with a boosted ego and can sleep peacefully, without having to admit what a piece of shit he is. A legend in his own mind."

After nursing an herbal tea for several hours while intently watching through the cafe's smoke-hazed windows, Officer Kilroy came stumbling out of the bar. He was being held up over the shoulder of another bar patron. The friendly stranger confirmed with the inebriated officer that he would be okay, then went back into the bar, leaving Officer Kilroy to stumble into the nearby alley. Alecia rolled her eyes in disgust when the officer opened his zipper and began urinating on the opposite wall of the alley. She was thankful that he was facing away from her at this angle. The relieved officer zipped his fly up, then teetered forward, leaning his face and chest against the wall about a foot above the highest part of the urine stain he had just left. The Officer went limp and his body slowly slid sideways, deeper into the alley until it flopped to the ground hard, swallowed by shadows. Alecia stared across the street, wide-eyed. After about 3 minutes she started to worry. If Kevin had gotten back up and continued down the alley, he may have found another way out and Alecia would have wasted her evening following him. If he was dead or dying of alcohol poisoning there would be no answers to the questions that she had.

Alecia kept a steady eye on the alley as she cautiously left the cafe' and with a brisk pace, raced across the street and then slowly approached the alley that she'd just seen Officer Kilroy disappear into. The sun had long since set while the Officer had been in the bar, leaving most of the alley an ink black mystery that would have to be explored up close to be understood. Alecia had expected to see Kilroy's feet just out of the glow of the street lights that still highlighted the glistening urine stain in the wall. She had begun to kick around, searching the darkness before her eyes had adjusted. Surprising herself when her foot made contact with nothing but asphalt and brick. "Where the hell had Kilroy gone?" Alecia wondered. If he'd crawled away out the other side of the alley and caught a cab, she was going to be pissed. As the off-duty officer searched her pocket for the tactical flashlight, a sound had answered the question that her light had not yet illuminated.

"You've been following me, Alecia," a familiar voice hissed from somewhere in the deep shadows. The voice was laced with a disturbing intensity, dropping the facade of being intoxicated. Alecia swallowed hard, her instincts telling her that she was in danger. "Kevin, I was just happening by when I saw you fall over, I wanted to make sure you're okay." "Happened by?" Kevin's disembodied voice continued from the shadows, "That's what you call waiting outside my barracks and then watching me from across the street for three hours?" "Shit, he knows." Alecia thought, considering that maybe she was just not as good as she thought at tailing someone without getting spotted.

Alecia turned, flipping on her flashlight and pointing it in the direction that the voice seemed to be coming from. The light fell across Kevin's face, momentarily blinding him as he raised a hand to help shield his eyes before adjusting. "Kevin, I just wanted to know what's going on. Something's not right."

A wicked grin spread across Kevin's face, and Alecia realized with a sinking feeling that she had stumbled upon something she wasn't meant to know. "You want to know, Alecia? Fine, I'll tell you." His tone turned eerily seductive. "But first, you have to do something for me."

"No, Kevin," Alecia asserted herself, leary of any favor this man would ask for. "If you're up to something that takes this much secrecy, I'm sure that I won't want to be a part of it."

Kevin's expression darkened, and in a sudden, terrifying motion, he pulled a gun from his jacket, pointing it at Alecia. Her breath caught in her throat as she stared down the barrel of the weapon. "Well then, I guess I just have to ask you to stand still." Kevin's voice got louder as he spoke, signaling that there was some sort of internal struggle that he was losing with his temper. Alecia did the opposite of what Kevin had requested, cutting her light, causing him to pause long enough for his eyes to adjust, giving her a split second to dive behind a nearby dumpster and out of the line of fire.

"Listen, Alecia," Kevin spat out, his voice trembling with madness. "You don't understand. We were meant to be together, I want you to be a part of me, and you ruined everything. But now, I can fix it. All you have to do is stop fighting it and you can see how good we can be together."

Alecia's mind raced as fear coursed through her veins. She had to get away from Kevin before he did something irreversible. If he shot her and left her for dead in an alley, fixing all of this with a time jump might suddenly not be an option. She turned and sprinted down the alley, her heart pounding in her chest.

Gunshots echoed behind her, and a searing pain ripped through her shoulder as a bullet struck her. She cried out in pain but forced herself to keep running, the adrenaline pushing her forward. Kevin's crazed pleas followed her, growing more desperate with each passing moment. "Alecia...come back...you don't understand..."

Alecia did all she could to ignore the danger behind her and keep moving, warm blood trickling down her left arm and dripping onto the ground. Her arm was numb and hard to bend, mostly hanging limply at her side. Her left shoulder emitted searing pain from both sides, the bullet having passed cleanly through her shoulder, but definitely damaging a nerve. Alecia gripped the shoulder with her right hand while she ran, trying to apply pressure that would stop her from bleeding out and also stop the trail that she was leaving.

She was mentally mapping the area that she'd walked just a few hours before, trying to determine the best series of streets and darkened alleys that she could take to lose Kevin and get to her car. She knew that she wouldn't be able to climb the ladder to its rooftop parking location, but if she could put enough distance between her and Kevin, she could buy enough time to summon the autopilot and have the car lower itself to her at street level.

"Alecia, come back!" The tense voice of an unraveling Kevin broke Alecia's mind out of her planning. "I'm sorry, I just want to talk."

The voice was too close for comfort, Alecia made a calculated risk, ducking and running across the open end of an alley, lit by the light of the street. Another of Kevin's bullets exploded brick into dust just a couple feet above Alecia's head as her silhouette disappeared behind the building.

A beam of light cut through the alley and onto the ground. Kevin was calming his panic enough now to use his brain, following the blood trail that betrayed Alecia's path of travel. The explosion of brick a moment before had sent new motivation from Alecia's brain to her limbs, she sprinted as best she could without being able to use her arms, trying to put distance between herself and her crazed pursuer. Her hand was busy, trying to keep the wound as closed as possible, so that her body wouldn't just pump her life fluid out of her new holes as she ran.

"This isn't you Alecia..." Kevin was shouting at shadows, trying to convince his wounded target to show herself. Alecia wheezed behind a nearby garbage truck, parked in an alley. Her lungs burned and she needed time to regroup and catch her breath. The stench emanating from the vehicle did not help. The smell burned Alecia's nostril's right to the back of her sinuses, and she struggled to repress the urge to gag, not wanting to give up her position.

Whether it was her heavy breathing or struggle against the stench that gave her away, one of Kevin's bullets ripped though the truck tire closest to her, and she bolted, disappearing into the shadows with Kevin's voice still calling after her to give herself up.

Alecia's mind was starting to get hazy from blood loss, but out of the haze, under the street lights, she saw a group of young Los Angelinos laughing and talking, in various states of intoxication, walking home after a night of bar room shenanigans. Alecia's usual pride was gone, replaced by a thankfulness that some witnesses could at least give her the time she needed to escape the crazed, gun-toting lunatic that was pursuing her.

"Help!" Alecia called out. The startled pedestrians suddenly fell silent as the bloody and panting woman ran toward them from the mouth of a dark alley and into the light of the street. "Holy shit lady, what the hell do you do?" A young man in the group asked. "Omigod, she's been shot, sit down, we'll call an ambulance." A bossy young woman from the group said with concern. "No," Alecia retorted vehemently, knowing she didn't have time for a full explanation. "Some asshole with a gun is chasing me. Call the cops." Alecia didn't wait to converse with the group, but picked her pace back up, clinging to the shadowed building facades and doorways of the street. The building she'd parked the car on was in sight now, maybe a block away. She was going to get there, she had determined. "Holy shit." came the startled reaction of another person in the group of bystanders as the young woman who'd been concerned for Alecia dialed the police.

Half a block closer to her target, Alecia could just barely hear the murmur of the group as Kilroy exited the dark alley that she'd emerged from just moments before. "Oh, shit, he's a cop." Alecia could just barely hear the comment from one of the bystanders. "Don't worry, official police business, she's an escaped fugitive..." Kilroy's voice faded out as Alecia rounded the farthest corner of the building that held her escape vehicle, several stories above. Her head was still clear enough to strategize. It would take time for the car to slowly lower itself to street level. She knew Kilroy didn't know where she was parked, so it made sense to get some more distance and have the car come to her in one of the darkened sidestreets, where she might be able to avoid the notice of her pursuer.

Alecia pressed a button on her belt that activated the car's autopilot and signaled that she needed a pickup at her location. Alecia's lungs and legs were burning. She rounded the corner to the furthest, darkest side of the building from where she'd last seen Kilroy. She was grateful for the moment she had to lean her back against the wall and try to catch her ragged breath, and calm herself. Alecia was only marginally successful, as the forty anxiety-ridden seconds she spent watching her armored vehicle lower itself to her location felt like hours. She breathed a heavy sigh of relief as the car finally rested in front of her. She hit the button on the door with her good hand, causing it to open with a "whir" sound.

As she began to enter the vehicle, a bullet slammed into and ricocheted off the heavily armored door, sending a new pump of adrenaline through Alecia's body. She lept in, closing the door behind her and hitting the button on the dash that told the car to raise itself to flight level and await a destination. Alecia grabbed the standard med kit in the center console and quickly unwrapped a syringe, pre loaded with a green gelatinous substance, she grimaced as she inserted the tip of the needle into her wound, continuing as she squeezed the plunger, releasing the compound into the wound, which expanded to staunch the flow of blood. The sound of another bullet impotently ricocheting off of the car drew Alecia's attention. She looked down from the windshield to see a confused and panicked looking Kevin Kilroy standing in the street.

Some of the witnesses that she'd encountered had cautiously sauntered up the street, curious to see how the end of this real life pursuit would conclude. She saw mouths moving, and had the moment to register that one of the bystanders must have said something to the effect of "I think she's a cop too." before Kilroy turned and ran for the Time Force barracks.

Alecia, still panting, grabbed her com-device with her right hand and shouted into it. "Shot's fired, officer down, I repeat shots fired, officer down backup and medical assistance needed, Officer involved shooting with Officer's Hernandez and Kilroy, located across from Time Force barracks at Lucas and West 5th." Alecia closed her eyes in relief when the dispatcher's voice responded. "Confirmed Officer Hernandez, all available units to Lucas and West 5th, shots fired, officer down."

Alecia was glad that the majority of on-duty law enforcement and medical aides were about to swarm on the location, although she knew she wouldn't be there to see it. If Kevin intended to run to the rooftop garage and grab his vehicle for pursuit, he'd be too late. Either way, she'd mentioned his name and they could track his location in any of a dozen ways. He'd have to explain the call to a large number of very curious officers before he would be able to even consider following her.

Alecia wrapped a bandage around the wound in her shoulder. It had stopped seeping blood thanks to the artificial compound that kept the wound closed, but it still ached right through her chest, from one side to the other, like she'd been stabbed with a hot fireplace poker. Finally, accepting that she'd survived the experience, Alecia slumped in her seat and broke down into heavy sobs, her car continuing to rise vertically as lights and sirens from across the city lit up the sky, coming to converge on the crime scene below.

After the moment of tense relief, clarity began to return to Alecia's mind, and with clarity, soon followed panic. If the authorities could track and question Kilroy, they'd also be following up the same way for her. Alecia didn't need to sleep on her next course of action any longer. She punched the address of the Project Magenta compound into the car's nav system, breathed heavily and slumped into the seat, exhausted and ignoring a silent trickle of tears still flowing from her eyes.

A moment later, Alecia's disheveled form startled awake, disoriented and unsure of her surroundings. The momentary lapse had only erased her recent memories temporarily, before her injuries reminded her of the reality of her situation. Unlike time travel, falling asleep in the present gave her no relief from pain or change of location.

Minutes later, Alecia was wiping her face with gauze from the med pack and composing herself as the docking arm took hold of her car for parking. Her arm, still weak at her side and throbbing in pain flopped limply as she jumped out of her car and sprinted to the open lift in the garage, avoiding her usual stairs. There was no time for delay, as Alecia knew that regardless of how Kevin explained himself, law enforcement would soon be tracking and converging on her point. An officer was reported down and when they determined that it clearly wasn't Kevin, the whole on-duty department would be looking to confirm her whereabouts and well-being, as well as ask a few questions.

Not wanting to waste any time Alecia took advantage of the open lift. I guess the military engineers of Project Magenta had never assumed that a Time Force officer would be crazy enough to jump out. Alecia was exactly that crazy, leaping out of the lift two floors above its target. She hit the floor hard, but rolled, lessening the impact to a sharp sting in her ankle. The rest in the car had afforded her the energy needed to regain her footing and continue at a brisk pace, but not much else. The lift froze behind her and a silent red light spun, signaling that the lift had suddenly realized it was devoid of passengers without reaching the desired floor. An automatic safety feature that Alecia hadn't witnessed, as she was too busy scanning in through the automated security door.

Alecia's breath was getting heavy again and that tweaked ankle was insistent on drawing attention to itself, slowing her progress. The silent orange alarms began peering out of their hidden wall compartments as she stumbled into the locker room. Clearly the authorities had flagged her and the building's automated computers had detected her presence. For all she knew, the entirety of law enforcement in Los Angeles was a minute, maybe two, behind her. Alecia commanded her sore, injured limbs to keep moving. When a surprised Dr. Gail Agu popped in from the Time Lab entrance, Alecia knelt to the ground on one knee and began to weep.

"Oh my lords!" Gail exclaimed at the sight for her friend. "What the Hell happened to you Alecia?". Gail knelt next to her wounded friend, placing a comforting hand on her wounded shoulder. Gail noticed the bandage just in time to make sure it was a very delicate comforting touch, gingerly avoiding the wound. She looked at the bloody bandage and then looked at Alecia, wide-eyed. "W...What..." Gail stammered, losing her voice to bewilderment before she could articulate the sentence in her mind.

Alecia sobbed heavily. "Gail, I fucked up, I really fucked up, I changed something, I changed something in the past." "What do you mean?" Gail asked, face now filled with horror. "I had a husband Gail, I had a husband, I loved him so much, but now he's gone, he died and I don't know why," Alecia was going with the abbreviated version, as much to keep Gail on a need to know basis as it was to save time. "And now Kilroy is obsessed with me and he shot me," Alecia motioned to her arm wound. "It's all wrong and I have to fix it Gail!" The doctor, afraid of what they were talking about, stammered, "We..we can talk to the Time Director, see how..." "No, there's no time, Gail. It won't work, I have to jump now." Alecia's head sank in defeat sobbing heavily.

Gail stared at her friend's defeated and bloody frame for a moment, then grabbed her arms, lifting her to her feet. The doctor looked around nervously as she ushered her wounded friend into the Time Lab. "Come on we've got to hurry, security is already on it's way." Alecia took a moment for her astonishment to clear and for what was happening to sink in. Her friend and supervisor, whose morals more than rules dictated she never abuse time technology, was about to help her abuse time technology. By the time Alecia accepted the reality of the situation, Gail had escorted her almost the entire way to the platform. Alecia confirmed she was steady enough to continue on her own, so Gail released her hold, allowing her to rush ahead and activate the control panel. "Okay, breathe, try to put yourself together...how far do you need to go back?" Alecia, injured foot dragging on the metal grating, thought quickly. She just needed to go back far enough to stop this. To stop Kevin from whatever the hell had happened in this timeline. And to stop Dale from killing himself, if she could. "I don't know, before college?" Gail thought for a moment, doing some mental math, bobbing her head as if she was writing an equation on a white board that no one else could see, before turning back to the time settings panel. "Okay, it should be set. As close as I can get you, anyway." "Thank you, Gail." Alecia was emphatic.

The sounds of security, Time Officers and other officials had begun to echo from the locker room. Gail walked briskly toward the entrance, buying Alecia the few precious seconds needed for the time field to charge up with its pink, rippling energy. Gail waved her arms in the air, standing firmly as the swarm of officers approached her. "Excuse me folks, what do you think is going on here?"

A large burly security guard grabbed Gail's wrists, using the momentum to turn her arms behind her back and press her face into the wall as a dozen or more officers continued past. "Hey!" one yelled at Alecia. It was too late for any of them to be effective. Injured, beaten and exhausted, Alecia slumped over, flopping over the edge and into the waiting pink pond of the Time Well.

Chapter 11

Alecia awoke in her cramped college dorm room, the familiar surroundings of her first year in the time law enforcement University program greeting her. As she glanced around the room, a sense of nostalgia washed over her. The posters of iconic time machines and inspirational quotes adorned the walls, just as she remembered them. "Shit!" she thought. "Not far enough." Alecia knew she couldn't really blame Gail though, she'd had to make a quick estimate, and directed time travel wasn't exactly a perfected science.

A quick search on the infoweb confirmed that Dale, the love of her life, was still dead by his own hand in this timeline. Alecia took a moment to indulge in despondency, wondering if this jump would be useless. She laid in bed feeling defeated, debating on how she could best make use of her day to save the future. "Maybe I should just lay here in bed until the day is over and sort things out when I go back to the present." She really considered it.

She laid there, thinking over everything that had happened. Her Dale, the original one, and her life with him. Her experience being a mechanic turned Time Officer, and her encounters with Kevin. She reached for the shoulder that had been shot before her jump, rubbing it as if to confirm it was okay. That shoulder was perfectly fine now, but her mind could still remember the burning sting of her wounds in the future.

Kevin. "That son of a bitch." Alecia thought. One thing she did know was that in this timeline, on this day, he was somewhere on this campus. She might not be able to save Dale, but she could make sure that Kevin never developed his obsessive fixation on her. She wasn't going to kill him. She didn't know what she'd do, but she knew that her actions could change the future. They had before, but her previous experiences had all been inadvertent. Now she had some intention, a mission of her own choosing. Take down Kevin. Somehow.

She bolted out of her bed of misery with a new purpose, throwing her sheets aside haphazardly. In a few moments she'd stripped off her pajamas, rummaging through her armoire for the first thing she could find, resembling an outfit. When her roommate, a dark skinned goth girl named Clarissa came out of the bathroom, Alecia was already half dressed, pulling a pink camo top on. "Oh, hey, we're going to meet with the T.A. to take some study notes for the finals, you wanna come?" "No, sorry, no time." Alecia responded curtly as she slid on a pair of cargo pants. "Things to do today." Alecia was already taking a stride toward the door , then thinking again, stepped back toward the armoire and grabbed a ballcap from an upper shelf, just in case she needed to conceal herself, without looking like she was concealing herself. "Later." Alecia said, sliding on the cap and heading out the door, leaving her roommate in dumbfounded silence, wondering what could possibly be more important today than studying for the upcoming finals for their first year of University.

As Alecia quickly marched out of her dorm building, no destination in mind, her brain swirled with exactly how she would go about preventing the future version of Kevin who had nearly killed her in an alley. She knew she couldn't kill him. It wasn't that she thought his absence would adversely affect the future, so much as she didn't want to risk waking up in the present as a federal inmate. She was really beginning to start thinking about stuff like that. Her tiny actions had borne drastic changes so far. She was concerned that a major change might cause her to wake up in a future where she didn't have access to the Time Well at all, preventing her from fixing the mistakes she'd made.

What would she do and how would she do it? That was the question of her day. "I've got one day," she thought, "but I'm going to change that son of a bitch if it's the last thing I do." Navigating through the bustling campus of U.C. Berkeley, Alecia struggled to form a plan of how exactly she would complete the future-changing mission she'd envisioned. "Where would Kevin be?" she thought. She sat under a tree, shaded from the California sun, and pulled the tablet from her bag. So far the campus's wifi hadn't been affected by all this personal history changing she'd been up to. She searched the infoweb for Kevin Kilroy, but only got what she already knew and was publicly accessible. He was a student of the Berkeley Time Law Enforcement program just like she was. Alecia brainstormed, came up with nothing, and was just about to let the feeling of despair she'd endured in her bed that morning seep back in, when she stumbled upon an idea.

The last time she'd found Dale in the past, on this very campus, was when she went with what she knew, where the students would be. Alecia rolled her eyes, embarrassed that she'd had the answer she needed all along. Alecia quickly scrolled through her list of contacts and typed a message to her dorm mate, Clarissa. "Oh, hey, I might join you guys to study after all. Where are you meeting?" Alecia set down the device, anxiously staring at the message screen in the hopes that Clarissa wasn't so deep in study that she had her notifications turned off. A few minutes later the tablet released a "ding" noise, accompanied by a line of text on-screen. "We're in the food court, come on over! :)"

"Yes," Alecia thought to herself, knowing that if this attempt didn't lead to Kevin, it would lead to someone who would. Alecia tossed her tablet in her bag and made a short walk to the cafeteria thanks to her brisk pace. By the time she had reached the cafeteria, her stomach was beginning to rumble. A quick look at the day's menu met Alecia's satisfaction. She was soon wandering around the cafeteria, carrying a plate of wonderfully aromatic fish tacos and looking for her fellow students. Alecia was soon spotted by Clarissa, who waved to get her attention. The aroma of lime and cilantro wafted into the air as she set down the tray next to a collection of hungry, studying time law students. "I figured we'd need some study food." Alecia said goodnaturedly. The hungry students looked at the plate of tacos wide-eyed, as if Alecia had just set down the holy grail. Alecia was already hefting a taco of her own, as her classmates asked her if she was sure they could have one. Alecia could only nod her approval, cheeks filled from a large bite of her taco. She waved off the thanks from her fellow students with a hand, as if to say, "No problem", still swallowing a mouthful of grilled cod, lime crema and carrot slaw.

"So you decided to study with us after all?" Clarissa asked with a smile, gingerly choosing a taco from the tray. "Yeah…" Alecia said, realizing that she really hadn't thought of an explanation as to why she had so abruptly snubbed her friend's earlier offer. "Sorry I took off so quickly earlier…pre-exam nerves." Alecia gestured with a rubbing motion to her stomach. "Uh…had to work out some anxiety gas, but I'm fine now." "Tell me about it!" Clarissa responded, "I destroyed that bathroom this morning!" Chuckles erupted from the cluster of students enjoying their fish tacos together. "So you gonna take out your tablet to study?" her friend continued. "Yeah," Alecia stammered, studying actually being the furthest thing from her mind. What she really wanted was an opportunity to present itself that would allow her to royally screw over Kevin. Maybe she could give him a fake answer sheet to the exam with all the wrong answers. She knew it wouldn't be that easy though, so she took out her tablet, in an effort to keep up appearances. "Look normal, be cool, change as little as possible." She thought to herself. "The T.A. already left for another meeting." Clarissa's voice continued to break into Alecia's inner thoughts and reminded her that she had to function in the present moment. "But he gave us a list of material to study for the exam, you can copy it from me." Alecia thanked her smiling roommate as she handed over her tablet. Alecia munched away on a taco, half-heartedly tapping the info from her friend's tablet onto her own screen, knowing that she really didn't care much about this exam. Alecia did her best to sound nonchalant as she slowly tapped her screen, "So, hey, you guys know that Kevin guy in our class? I think his name is Kilroy?"

Alecia looked up to see Clarissa exchange a hesitant glance with another female student sitting across the table, munching on her own taco. "What?" Alecia asked, concerned that she'd missed some key detail about this timeline. Clariss lowered her head and raised her eyes to Alecia, speaking in a low tone, trying not to be overheard, but also concerned. "You don't have something going on with that guy, do you?" Alecia nearly choked on a bite of her second taco. "No, nothing like that, why?" "He's a jerk." Clarissa responded. The other student, mouth now free of tasty grilled fish, spoke up. "My friend in Environmental Science had a run-in with him. Apparently he doesn't like to take no for an answer." That sounded like the Kevin that Alecia knew. Alecia determined that she'd been worried about missing a major difference for nothing. The girls all shared a knowing disgusted look at each other over the familiar feelings they shared over having to deal with overly amorous men.

"He's right over there." the student across the table gestured with a roll of her head over one shoulder. Alecia's mouth stopped chewing involuntarily in surprise. There, not more than 30 yards away, was Kevin, surrounded by a small pack of students, watching him talk and gesture wildly, as if he was a professor giving an impromptu lecture in the dining hall. Alecia, realizing her mouth was blocked with her delicious lunch, finally remembered to chew and swallowed hard. She couldn't believe her luck. She knew she had to act, thought she had yet to form a plan. She looked at the object of her ire, back to her fellow students, back at Kevin, then back to her friends, then she rose from the table. Wiping the last of the lime sauce that had leaked on to her fingers, she leaned over to the girl that had been across the table from her and whispered, just loud enough for their little inner circle to hear "Tell your friend this is for her."

Alecia tossed her napkin in a nearby automated garbage receptacle, and casually strode toward Kevin and his gathering of disciples, keeping them in her peripheral. She gave a mischievous look back to her curious friends and a sly, confident wink. As she approached the gesticulating chauvinist her bravado faltered just a little. She still didn't know exactly what she was going to do.

"I'm telling you," Kevin boasted to his small audience, "Engineering, Mathematics, Environment, all of those people are going to regret their majors when all of us, the Time Force, fix all those problems and put them out of a job." Alecia chuckled to herself in her head at Kevin's amateur arrogance and misunderstanding of exactly how the Time Force worked. Having years, and multiple timelines of experience in her head, Alecia knew that everyone, not just the engineers and scientists that worked for the Time Force, made what they do possible, but that all professionals and walks of life had their roles to play in the improvement of the Time Force. What they did wouldn't be possible without engineers and environmentalists and mathematicians and a plethora of other job descriptions, right down to the janitor that was currently mopping a spill and shaking his head at what this little shit was spouting to his classmates. Alecia managed to pass by Kevin without being noticed so far. He was too busy with his performance.

"And we're gonna get so much pussaay!" Kevin made sure he said that last part loudly, for others outside of their crowd to hear, as he made a hard, thrusting gesture. Laughter and praise erupted from Kevin's audience as he raised his arms in the air in victory, basking in the glow of attention of his peers. He turned around as if to display himself to all in attendance, as if they'd come to hear him speak and not just needed study food for their own exams. As he turned, Alecia caught Kevin's eye. She'd almost made it undetected. Their eyes met and Kevin gave her a sleazy sideways grin and a wink.

"OH, shut the fuck up, Kevin." Alecia's mind popped, her unexpected response surprised Kevin and his cronies into momentary silence. "You think you're better than everyone, when you're really the worst of us. You say you want to change the world, but you really just want power and attention. You're pathetic!" Alecia realized that her loss of temper had worked in her favor and that she was on a roll, as sounds of "oh" and "Aww, damn" began to emanate from onlookers. "And as for any pussy you get, well, it's only going to be the unconscious kind, just like every other sexual encounter your sleazy date-rapping ass has ever had."

Kevin and Alecia stared at each other for a moment, his face turned three shades of angry red, betraying his silence, but saying nothing. Alecia gave a nod, letting Kevin know she had been happy to put him in his place and continued walking toward the cafeteria exit. Embarrassed, but looking to save face, Kevin turned back to his audience, arms spread. "Well what can I say? She must be on her..." Before Kevin could finish his sentence, Alecia had turned back and quickly scampered up behind him. With a quick motion she firmly gripped a belt loop on either side of his hip and tugged down hard. Before he had any idea what was happening, his pants were around his ankles. Kevin had also gone commando that day. Laughter, hoots and hysterics erupted from the entire food court, even the janitor. Shocked, Kevin scrambled to cover his genitals, tripping thanks to the restriction of the pants around his ankles and scrambling to pull his pants back up.

Alecia had already quickly scampered out of the dining hall. She exited the building and walked into the warm sun, grinning, proud of accomplishing her mission to take Kevin down a peg. She knew that he was not likely to report the incident, too embarrassing, but that it would definitely take him down a peg.

Alecia walked back to her dorm room, and stretched out on her bed. She pulled out her tablet, plugged in her earphones and hit a small word in the corner of the screen that said "audio". A pleasant voice began reciting the notes that Alecia had taken from Clarissa, something she always did when she studied. She rolled and smoked a joint, making sure to blow the smoke out of the window before relaxing into a warm, sun-laden afternoon nap, the voice in her ears, still reading off the basic tenets of time law enforcement.

Chapter 12

As Alecia emerged from the Time Well, a wave of shock and disbelief washed over her. The Time Force jumpsuit she now wore was nothing like the standard uniform she had grown accustomed to. Instead, it was a scandalously skimpy and sexualized version, revealing far more than it concealed. Alecia felt exposed and uncomfortable, her cheeks flushed with embarrassment. Her other cheeks were on full display as well.

The standard-issue belt, with holsters for gun, baton and taser were there, but everything else was different. She couldn't complain about the color, her bottoms were a deep, vibrant pink, but they were also bikini bottoms. They matched the knee-high vinyl boots. She also had matching knee and elbow pads along with dark gray tactical gloves. Her midriff and lower back were as exposed as her ass and thighs. Her chest was covered in a form-fitted metallic polymer body armor. Over her shoulders, made of the metallic polymer and attached to the body armor with a flexible black webbing material, were a pair of pink, triangular shoulder pads, each at least 2 feet wide. Still no helmet. "How the hell does this protect anybody?" Alecia muttered.

Her apprehension did not fade as she climbed the ladder, as the strange sound of a room full of voices, like a busy restaurant filled with conversations, became clearer the higher she climbed. She cautiously, apprehensively, peaked out over the edge of the pit, into the open Time Lab.

Her voice didn't come, but her face said "What the fuck?". Another gray gloved hand reached out and a friendly voice said "Welcome back, Officer Hernandez." Alecia looked up to see the warm, smiling face of a young, male officer staring back at her. He had a tan brown complexion and short hair with a spiky bang fringe, dyed blonde. He, like the other male officers in the room, wore a full-body padded gray suit, similar to the time jump uniform that she was familiar with. This Time officer's shoulder pads were yellow, which Alecia guessed signified that he was a trainee.

As Alecia rose into the time-lab, she was startled and slightly horrified by what she saw. Time Officers and scientists in lab coats milled about the room. The air was thick, as many of the attendees in the now cramped feeling lab were smoking various substances in hookah pipes, vapes and more. Many of the Time Officers were milling about, conversing loudly and carrying drinks. The female officers wore the same uniform as Alecia, except none of them had the fully matching pink aesthetic, sporting bikini bottoms of various colors, some had gone to the same trouble as Alecia, matching the colour of her shoulder pads, some hadn't. In some cases, female officers were draped across the laps of male officers, some in pairs, many shared a dazed look of euphoria from whatever substance they were currently enjoying. The male officers wore the same uniform as the young man who had just helped her out of the pit. Shoulder pads seemed to indicate rank, running the spectrum from yellow, to orange, to deep pink and finally red. "At least I'm the second highest rank," Alecia thought to herself. If she was a senior officer, she could expect that some of this farcical behavior would be below her station. There were only two officers wearing red shoulder pads, both were male. For the most part the senior officers with the red shoulder pads sat silently watching, female officers draped on and around them, passing by and flirting, making suggestive comments. One of the red officers finally cracked a grin and made a low murmur to one of his female admirers that said he had just made a well-received suggestive comment in return. Several staff members wandered through the room in formal attire, apparently waiters of some type, bringing food, drink and drugs to those who desired it.

The scene was indulgent, and not like any timeline that Alecia had encountered thus far. The entire room had an air of indulgence and hedonism that was utterly alien to her.

"Did you achieve your mission objective?" The fresh faced officer asked a bewildered Alecia. "Yes," Alecia bluffed absentmindedly, not wanting to say anything to betray her time-altering efforts. "Interesting," the officer responded, "there's a huge chronal radiation spike, but it doesn't seem to have affected the cost of producing opium." Alecia fumbled for what to say, failing to maintain a nonchalant air, as her mind began to process what she was being told. "Oh well, we'll just keep trying. Did you accomplish any personal objectives?" the upbeat Officer asked. "Yeah..." Alecia responded hesitantly. "Well then it wasn't a waste right?" the Time officer responded, "I'm gonna try and give myself some details that will help me move up ranks faster on my next jump." With that, the young officer turned to a plate of cocaine moving by, held aloft by one of the "waiters". His head beant, making a loud "SNORT" sound, as he sucked a thin line of cocaine into one nostril. The officer beamed a grin at Alecia and walked off to join the other officers, lounging about.

Alecia stood in silence, not sure what to do. She was in a timeline that made no sense. How could her actions, how could pantsing Kevin in a university dining hall, have made this timeline? Her mind felt like it was about to collapse under the weight of just how different the world had become since she had embarked on the mission to save Dale. After a moment of stunned silence, taking it all in, Alecia realized that she had caught the attention of the two red shoulder-padded officers, who were eyeing her suspiciously as other female Time Officers continued to fawn over them. Alecia wasn't sure what they had been expecting her to do, but she knew she wouldn't be doing that. Before she could recompose a facade of normalcy, a paige girl in a monokini entered the time lab and spoke "Announcing the arrival of your hero and mine, our supreme magistrate, the Time Director!"

Six large, muscled, yellow shoulder-padded Time Officers marched into the room behind her, each holding one side of a polished brass rod with a big round brass knob on the end. The three brass rods ran through the base of a small platform, covered in decorative colorful rugs. Atop the platform sat a large blue and red chair, a throne really. And on the throne sat Kevin Kilroy. Alecia recognized him right away. The ridiculous hair, the shit-eating grin, the lecherous smirk. He held a large glass of wine up in one hand in recognition of the cheers of his arrival. He wore the same uniform as the other Time Officers, except his red shoulder pads were bisected by two wide white stripes on either side, indicating his superior rank to all others.

The entire room had turned to see and cheer for Kilroy's arrival. Alecia was frozen in silent horror.

After a few moments that seemed like hours, Alecia was unable to contain her outrage any longer, her voice cutting through the debauchery that surrounded her. "This is all wrong! Everything about this timeline is a nightmare!"

Her words were met with a chilling silence, broken only by murmurs of disapproval and disdain. It was clear that she had crossed a line, challenging the established order of this nightmarish reality. In an instant, she regretted her impulsive outburst. Time Director Kilroy held Alecia's gaze for a moment, then spoke with a sneer "Enemy of the State!"

As the echo of Kilroy's words faded, the room erupted into chaos.

Time Officers loyal to Time Director Kilroy surged forward, a horde of menacing figures determined to capture Alecia. Panic coursed through her veins as she turned and fled, running down once familiar corridors, alarms blaring. By the time Alecia reached a security gate her heart was pounding in her chest. The lone guard watched wide eyed as the woman barreled toward him, followed by a wave of angry time agents in pursuit. Thinking quickly Alecia jumped over the barricade turnstyle, striking the surprised guard before he could finish raising his automatic weapon. While still stunned from the hit, Alecia wrenched his weapon from his grasp and struck him hard across the face, leaving him unconscious and slumped to the ground. A quick glance at the world outside revealed something far different than she'd ever experienced in her life, or even the altered timelines. Similar to the tent city and homeless neighborhood that she'd encountered after her first jump, tents, tarps and ragged people reached as far as the eye could see. Alecia was horrified when it sank in to her that this was likely how the whole city was now. She had no time to contemplate further, as the wall of angry co-workers was climbing over the turnstiles. She dropped the gun and ran into the vast sea of tarps and tattered clothes on laundry lines.

She had to admit, these Time Officers were determined, shouts of "Halt" and "We are hunting a fugitive" rang out behind her. She kept up her pace enough that she could see the look of recognition on the dirty faces hiding in the shadows, but was long gone before any of them could decide if they wanted to help the police in their pursuit. Aside from a couple of close calls, where some crafty Time Officers lunged at her from between tents, attempts she quickly dodged, she was able to put a good distance between her and her pursuers, dodging and weaving through the massive maze of a homeless camp. With each step, she pushed herself harder, determined to maintain her freedom long enough to figure out how she was going to fix this all.

As she rounded a corner and bolted down another pedestrian pathway, the wall panel of a ramshackle shed made of sheet metal swung open in front of her. A shabbily dressed arm held the panel open and a voice from inside said "get in!".

Chapter 13

Alecia's heart pounded in her chest unsure if she had just stepped into a greater danger than she was fleeing from. A handily designed spring pulled the metal panel she'd entered through back into place. She hid in the shadows of a decaying building, pressed against the dirty, rusted metal wall. A single bulb dangled from a wire, swinging in space, creating deep shadows that obscured the details of her potential rescuer, save for the tattered rags and hood that covered them. The stranger's hand reached up and the lower part of his face emerged enough from the shadows to make a "Shh" gesture with a finger. Alecia understood right away and decided that she would continue to cooperate, as long as it seemed that the danger outside was greater than the danger in her shadowy hiding place.

The stranger leaned toward the wall, peeking through rusted cracks and listening intently. After the shouts of pursuing officers had passed and faded into the tent city, the stranger didn't move, frozen, as if not trusting his own ears. After a few more excruciating seconds the hooded figure nodded, as if finally confirming to himself it was safe to move. Wordlessly, the mysterious figure stepped backward into the light and pulled down his hood, revealing a surprising face. His red mohawk had grown out, making most of it a shiny, dark black, except for the tips, and his face was more wrinkled and haggard than she had seen before, but this was the familiar face of Officer Frank Morgan.

"Frank!" Alecia blurted out. The man smiled at the recognition "yes," he responded, "I can tell you're a little surprised that I'm the face of the resistance." "Yeah...I...but..." Alecia stammered, unsure of where to start or what to say to explain how she had come to need rescuing in this timeline. "Don't worry, there's plenty of time to talk once we get to a secure position." It was then that Alecia realized the shadows in the cramped metal space were moving. Several other raggedy hooded figures, rebels she assumed, had been waiting and watching, just outside of the light of the single bulb. Suddenly the sound of rattling metal overhead was followed by a large, stark beam of daylight assaulting the eyes of those inside the sheet metal building. A lanky form quickly jumped down through a rooftop port hole, closing it behind them in a fluid motion as they entered and landing in their midst. The figure stood and to Alecia's surprise, revealed itself to be the smiling, yellow shoulder-padded trainee who had greeted her on her most recent climb out of the Time Well. "They've ended the pursuit, but there will be squads assigned for a more thorough search soon, we need to move."

"Great job making yourself a fugitive Officer Hernandez." the officer grinned "We usually try to keep things down low and undercover, but welcome to the resistance." There was something about this man's complexion, and his eyes, that tugged on Alecia's memory, but she couldn't quite place it. Before Alecia could get lost in searching for the answer in her mind Officer Morgan stepped forward once again. "We need to move." was all he said, leaving Alecia to figure out that she should follow this new group of dishevelled strangers as they began to move across the metal shack in unison. They entered what looked like a cinder block hallway. As she caught up with them and the group moved into the musty tunnel, a string of lights dangling from a cord that was fastened to the wall illuminated the figures and faces, allowing more detail to be seen. Some of the group of roughly seven people wore Time Officer uniforms under their rags, like Officer Morgan. Others appeared to be members of the poor population of the tent city, no uniform under their rags. All had dirty, weary faces, tired from waging a rebellion that Alecia could only imagine. The group walked for what felt like several miles in a steady direction. Without reference Alecia couldn't be sure, but she felt like the tunnel was sloped downward on a very gradual, but noticeable decline. They must have been going literally deeper underground.

Just as the lactic acid build-up in her thighs began to burn from her earlier run, in a way that told her that she'd soon need to rest, the yellow padded trainee, no tatters covering his uniform, approached Alecia. "That was amazing, the way you called out Kilroy," he said excitedly, "Suicidal, but amazing." Alecia stared at the man's features and the puzzle pieces in her head finally fit into place. She knew why this man looked so familiar "Gabriel?" Alecia blurted out, "Gabriel Yoshawa?" "Whoa!" the Officer grinned, "You read my file? I didn't even think you knew my name, or remembered who I was." He said excitedly. "When it comes to rebellion, us Lake Tahoe kids gotta represent." Gabriel, Gabriel Jr. actually, chuckled. Alecia was stunned, not only by the fact that Dale's older, estranged brother was a Time Officer in this timeline, but that he was very different from the haggard, brooding man she had only encountered a few times in her original timeline.

Before she could follow up with more questions, Gabriel sprinted ahead, to where Officer Morgan was beckoning for assistance. Alecia looked down the tunnel but saw nothing to indicate any change in circumstances or direction, just a long tunnel extending for miles into the darkness. The two men approached an unassuming and nondescript section of cinder block wall. Together they shoved against it. There was a metallic clanging noise and a section of wall shifted backward, revealing the outline of a large doorway. The pair slowly pushed the panel, sliding it to the side and allowing access to a dark open space beyond. Morgan and Yoshawa gestured for the group, including Alecia, to move into the room quickly before they each gripped a wall-mounted iron bar, which helped them put the panel back into place.

Officer Morgan grabbed a metal latch, pulling it down and locking the brick panel back into place with a loud thud that echoed through the room. The act of locking the secret door seemed to trigger a faint buzzing sound that filled the room. The sound rose into an audible hum, several computer screens and ceiling mounted lights flickered to life.

The room itself was clearly once part of the Los Angeles sewer system. The pungent smell of old human waste still hung in the air and stung the back of your nostrils. By some miracle of development planning, or maybe purposeful man-made one, this section of sewer no longer had the waste of the people of Los Angeles flowing through it. A series of metal rails and grating had been bolted into the brick and concrete, allowing for a meeting table, several computerized work stations, and some "flop areas" filled with old couches and furniture for members of the rebellion to use during meetings.

Officer Morgan took a seat at the head of the table and gestured openly with his arms. "Welcome to the rebellion, Hernandez." "I told you guys we should be more open to recruiting new members," Chimed Gabriel Yoshawa Jr. Officer Morgan shot Yoshawa a skeptical, sideways look of disagreement before continuing, "You may be wondering why myself and other Time Officers would be involved in rebelling against a system where we can literally go back in time and make our lives better any time we want. The answer to that is that we shouldn't, because it makes the world worse for everyone else in it, every time we do..." "We believe that Time Technology should have never been used for anyone's personal gain, but for the betterment of all of society." Yoshawa interrupted. "Right," Morgan continued. "Not only that, we believe that the selfish changes of the ruling class have changed our present from what it once was, and what it was supposed to be." Alecia listened intently, unsure whether she should interject to explain to the rebels how right they were. "In fact, we believe that someone with access to time travel has been making drastic changes, manipulating history and society in major ways for their own benefit, we're just not sure who." "As if we don't have any good ideas though," Yoshawa interjected. Morgan gestured with open hands that Yoshawa should continue, if he wanted. "Ever since President Kilroy took office, things have gone to shit..." "What? PRESIDENT Kilroy?" It was now Alecia's turn to interrupt in disbelief. "Yes," Yoshawa continued, "As we all know, ever since Leonard Kilroy ran and pulled off a stunning upset victory to become the president, the quality of life for the average USDNA citizen has plummeted. Those close to the president and in power have continued to experience unbelievable luck and prosperity, while Kilroy himself has appointed those closest to him into the highest positions of power. That includes the meteoric rise of his son, Kevin Kilroy, to the head position of Time Director of the Time Force." "That's right," it was Officer Morgan's turn to resume the explanation. "It might sound like some crazy shit from an old sci-fi movie, but we believe that our current timeline has been drastically changed by nefarious interests for their own personal gain, the cost of which is being paid by the populace. We can't pinpoint exactly who for sure, the extent of the changes are impossible to pinpoint to one person, but we know it's someone currently in our ruling class. In short, the world is not what it was, nor what it was meant to be."

Alecia's stomach balled up into a knot. If there was ever a time to break her vow of silence about her time altering experiences, it was now. "I...think I should tell you guys something." Alecia stammered. "I've been keeping it all to myself and the memories are starting to overwhelm my mind, I can't tell what really happened and what didn't anymore."

With trepidation, Alecia told her story to the stunned silent, dirty faces of the rebellion that were present. The whole story. Even back to Dale and his battle with cancer and her misguided attempt to bring him back. After her story ended, the room fell silent. Faces exchanged furtive glances until Officer Morgan finally spoke. "Well, this does give us some new information to work with..."

"I'm so sorry." Alecia blurted out, nearly bursting into tears under the weight of her guilt. "It's all my fault."

"I don't believe it is." Officer Morgan tried to reassure her. "From all that you've said, I don't think your actions could have caused the changes we've seen. You may have broken the rules, but there is no way that we could isolate which Time Force officer is causing changes, when we have dozens jumping back every day, doing things to make life better for themselves."

"So what's the plan, boss?" Gabriel Yoshawa Jr. chimed in.

"Well," Morgan responded. "Of anyone we have available, it now appears that Hernandez has the closest connection to any timeline outside of this shit show. She should be the one to jump, if possible."

"She's been declared a fugitive." Yoshawa interjected. "How do we get her anywhere near the time lab?"

"That's a good question." Morgan thought for a moment. Alecia stood in silence, constantly on the verge of saying...something, but the thoughts and memories swirling in her head were too overwhelming to form words. "Our best bet is to take her in, Yoshawa and myself, say we want an interrogation room, then raid the lab before security can catch on."

"What about this?" a dirt faced rebel wearing tattered robes hefted a transparent tablet in front of him. On the screen a 3-dimensional scan of Alecia's head rotated with the word "WANTED" in bold letters above it. The notification also offered a $4,000,000 reward for her capture, alive or dead.

"Even with us in uniform, that much money being offered? We'll never make it to the compound with her, once she's recognized." Yoshawa said dejectedly.

"You're not wrong." Morgan responded, deep in thought for a moment before continuing. "We disguise her. We make her look like one of the homeless, a random prisoner, until we get inside." Alecia exchanged nervous glances with the other faces in the room as Morgan formulated his plan in real time. "I want the rest of you to follow us at 100 yards distance, don't act unless we run into trouble. Spread the word, Alpha, Omega and Zeta units be prepared and ready if called upon to help. We get in as quickly and quietly as possible. Alecia should jump, but if something happens, in the worst case scenario she can't, myself or Yoshawa can jump in her place. It wouldn't be ideal, but it's really the only move we have."

Morgan's words rang in Alecia's ears. She knew that "worst case scenario" was code for "if she can't jump because she's dead,". She couldn't help but wonder what would happen if she didn't make it. Would her time traveling exploits be over? Would the chance of ever returning to the world that she knew end when her life was extinguished?

"So my brother married the chick that stole his cigarettes on the school bus?" Officer Yoshawa, the new one, at least to Alecia, broke the tension with his characteristic smile and upbeat demeanor. His question pulled Alecia's mind out of the pit of self-pity she'd been sinking into. "That's not exactly how it worked..." Alecia responded with a light chuckle, "...but for simplicity's sake, yes." "Well then, let's get you back to him," Yoshawa said, maintaining the happy-go-lucky tone that he seemed to approach all things with. "When do we go, boss?" Yoshawa's face turned to Morgan as he asked the question with an exuberance usually reserved for children asking about going to an ice cream shop.

Morgan thought for a beat, then looked sternly at his gathered people. "With Kilroy and those loyal to him having unrestricted access to the Time Well, the only time to go is now."

As the weight and immediacy of Morgan's words sank in, a member of the rebellion stepped forward, handing a pair of yellow lensed goggles to Alecia. She took the goggles tentatively and nodded a "thank you" to the donor. One by one, the members of the rebellion stepped forward, donating pieces of their own garb to Alecia's disguise. When it was all said and done, Alecia wore an air filtration mask over her face, along with the yellow goggles. Her skimpy Time Force uniform was covered in tattered rags, and a thick frayed hood that would help obscure others from getting a good look at her. The officers placed a wide leather belt with several metal rings attached to it around her waist, standard for transporting a fugitive by foot. The officers would each connect a tether to one of the metal rings. The belt also served to keep her tattered robes in place, helping to reduce the chance of being exposed and recognized.

The old rags smelled. They'd been soaked in human grease and sweat more than once, the smell of human body odor mixing with a number of other mystery materials that the fabrics had come into contact with at one time or another. Alecia suppressed the urge to gag, knowing that some of these people had donated one of very few items they owned in order to help her remain undetected. She would have to do her best to blend in until she was well inside the Project Magenta compound. The air mask helped a lot, but it wasn't able to filter out all of the sour odors that stung the back of Alecia's throat.

The group exited the secret lair, moving deeper down the dimly lit cinder block tunnel for about 500 yards then turned left, into a disused circular sewer tunnel that crossed the mysterious hallway. They followed the sewer about a mile before climbing up a ladder one-by-one that led into the inside of a large empty wooden crate. Officer's Morgan and Yoshawa flipped open the crate lid from inside and cautiously exited, soon followed by Alecia and the rest of their rag tag group. The crate that camouflaged the sewer entrance sat in the far corner of a modest, slightly dilapidated living room. Elderly citizens of Los Angeles, leather-skinned street urchins, occupied several small tables on the edges of the room. Some played cards, others were working on a game of backgammon. One pair was playing an old fashioned game of checkers. Not a single one of them looked up from their game at the group of rebels moving through their home, as if this was just a normal part of everyday life. Nor did they look up at the wall mounted screen that continued to broadcast the day's news, including the search for Alecia.

They approached a dilapidated wooden door, cracks between the boards allowed the outside sunlight to stream in. Morgan made a quick, furtive peak out of one of the cracks in the boards, and seemed satisfied with what he saw. Officer's Morgan and Yoshawa took one final look over Alecia, making sure that her ragged outfit covered any detail that could betray her true identity. Yoshawa took hold of one of Alecia's wrists, slapped a cuff on it and positioned it around her back. "This is just for appearances," he explained. "The left shackle isn't coupled, in case we get into trouble and you need your hands freed quickly." Alecia couldn't argue with the jovial Time Officer's attention to detail. Each officer attached a retractable cord from their belt to a metal loop on the leather belt placed around Alecia's robes. Morgan gave a stern look. "Are you ready?" he asked, with a gaze that felt as if it was boring into Alecia's soul. She breathed deeply and responded "Yes." "Good," Frank Morgan said, "we need to get you to the Time Well now!" With that, Morgan kicked open the wooden door, allowing the light of day to pour in while he stepped into the open world of Los Angeles's tent city.

Alecia was momentarily blinded, as the Officers attached to her by belt cables hefted their firearms and walked ahead of her. "Make way. We're transporting a prisoner." She heard Morgan's voice order the disheveled bystanders before her eyes had finished adjusting to the light, even with the protection of her goggles. The California sun beat down mercilessly, which in turn caused heat to rise from the asphalt, concrete and brick that had once been the streets that wheeled vehicles traveled the city, leaving the residents of tent city to feel as if they were being cooked from both directions. Now the city streets had been long covered in tents and ramshackle dwellings of the destitute, attempting to escape the heat or offer the small comfort of a patch of shade. Above the haphazard tarpaulin dwellings, large video screens were mounted on the exterior walls of the city's oldest and tallest buildings. Any person who wasn't too downtrodden to look up would have at least one viewable screen. Every single screen showed the fugitive notice of Officer Alecia Hernendez, wanted for treason. She had become a fugitive in this twisted reality, forced to rely on her wits and the kindness of strangers to survive.

Alecia did her best not to stare at the screens and blow their cover, trying to keep her head down and out of the view of curious onlookers. Her mind reeled at the vastness and cramped condition of the tent city, as she and her fake captors slowly squeezed through miles of ragged, sweaty and closely packed bodies. Morgan and Yoshawa would occasionally order the peasants to move when the throng of people got so tightly packed that even the Time Force officers had trouble making way on the authority of their appearance alone. Soon the heat of the sun was penetrating Alecia's soiled and tattered robes, causing unpleasant odors to release and mix with the stale, hot air around her. Soon her own sweat was soaking into the fibers and adding to the rankness of her garments. Alecia continued to be thankful that some rebel had been generous, or knowing enough, to donate that breathing mask.

The trio proceeded through the tent city slowly, and as Alecia's mind began to wander, not just about all of her experiences, but exactly how she would handle herself, the Project Magenta compound came into view in the distance. She realized that she'd lost sight of their trailing backup in the throng of people, which made her uneasy, even as she convinced herself that they were still there and watching for any trouble.

A moment later, the prisoner and her apparent captors passed a sharp eyed peasant, who ducked his head, taking a peak at the prisoner apparently being led by two Time Officers. Alecia felt her hood suddenly pulled back, her shock of pink hair new exposed and betraying her identity. "The fugitive is here!" the man bellowed to all who would listen. His surprisingly strong hand grabbed Alecia's shoulder, spinning her around to face him and the throng of curious and onlookers. Alecia looked at the man. He had the appearance and large frame that was not unlike a troll. Long, dark. scraggly hair framed his head and hung limply down to his chest, matching the large matted black beard that nearly reached up to his eyes, which of course rested under a matching set of bushy, overgrown black eyebrows. Alecia momentarily considered how much this man looked like a smaller version of the "Sweetums" character from the Muppets, a vintage comedy puppet show that her mother had shown her recording files of as a child. Alecia could tell just by looking at this man that he was likely more than she could handle in a physical confrontation. The grip on her shoulder confirmed that idea.

"This is our prisoner!" Yoshawa bravely stepped forward, attempting to get between the man and Alecia. Murmurs of recognition were beginning to rise out of the throng of desperate and poor watching the confrontation. "This is my four million dollars!" the man bellowed back, shoving Yoshawa back with his free hand. Yoshawa quickly recovered his balance, but not before the troll had made use of the split-second. Enough to produce a cattle-prod like taser from inside of his threadbare robes. The man took a defensive stance toward the Time Officers, confident that the prisoner that he intended to turn in for the reward himself was actually restrained.

Before the hairy troll man could confirm that Alecia actually was restrained, she quickly ducked out of his grip and extended her arm as she spun. The loose, pointed end of her open shackle dug into the man's cheek like a fish hook, exiting the sharp end out through his mouth. Blood sprayed from his surprised mouth and the shackle poked out from between his teeth. Alecia quickly used her free hand to punch the man square across the jaw, only momentarily stunning him off balance, but loosening his grip enough for Alecia to yank the baton from his hand. She quickly pressed the blue, glowing end into the tangle of robes. The troll-like man uttered another pained groan before his immense weight carried him unconscious to the ground, ripping Alecia's improvised stabbing tool through his face and free of his now mangled flesh.

Alecia, Yoshawa and Morgan all had a brief moment to exchange glances with each other and at the faces of the bewildered and desperate poor that surrounded them. Officer Morgan issued his order, "Run!".

Morgan, Yoshawa and Alecia began frantically pushing oblivious bystanders out of the way, looking for openings that would allow them to pick up speed in their approach to the compound, now that the advantage of surprise had been lost to them. The occasional opportunist would try their luck in the hopes of wrestling a payday from the officers. Those that tried were quickly taken out with fists and elbows, as well as the handy taser wand that Alecia now possessed. Cries began to rise up from the throngs of disheveled citizens around them. "Capture her!" "Traitor" "Time criminal!" and other disembodied voices rolled out of the impersonal mass of people and to the rebels ears. They pressed forward. A gunshot caught their ears, giving Alecia pause to look back in fear. Her apprehension passed as she realized it was the remaining group of rebels, fighting off the choking crowd, scuffling and pushing through in an attempt to get closer and offer assistance. Morgan turned back, grabbing Alecia's arm and pulling her forward. "We don't have time to stop!"

The trio pressed forward on their own, trying in vain to get ahead of the wave of recognition spreading through the crowd and being whispered into weather-beaten tents and shanties. As a throng of merchants moved their carts out of the market area, packing up for the day, a relatively open path to the compound emerged ahead of them. Panting, muscles burning, the three comrades sprinted toward the Project Magenta security gates and the pair of armed guards stationed there.

The hope spurred on in the hearts of the rebels began to melt, as they were closing in on the gate, within twenty yards, six more armored guards filed out to join their two comrades. All eight raised their automatic weapons, leveled at the three battle-worn rebels, whose plan to change time appeared to be going sideways quickly. "Halt" commanded a voice from behind a guard's helmet. The action and scuttlebutt of the crowd had subsided, replaced with a fear of the armed authorities. Officer Frank Morgan thought for a moment, lowered his weapon and shouted "We have the fugitive, she is our prisoner and we intend to question her."

"Then why is she not restrained?" the apparent representative of the guards responded. "Look at this mob." Morgan attempted to reason. "We had to let her defend herself or she wouldn't have made it here alive!" "With no report in ahead? From a senior officer?" the guard responded. "You hand her over to us and leave, we'll take her in for questioning."

Morgan's face lowered. He looked down, breathed in and then out with a heavy stressful sigh and back up again, his surprise replaced by a cold seriousness. "Ad Astra Per Aspera!" Morgan shouted the latin phrase as if he was a legendary general rallying troops on an ancient battlefield. Guards, homeless and Alecia alike stood in silence, wondering what the significance of Officer Morgan's actions actually was. Morgan began to look nervous as the uncomfortably long silence continued. "Ad Astra Per Aspera!" A small chorus of voices rang out in response finally. There was a rustling among the clothes lines and battered tarps of the tent city, as well armed rebels began to emerge from tents and other hiding places nearby, joining the ranks of the three Time Officers who were attempting to storm the military compound. As the call echoed through the throng of impoverished, Morgan, Alecia and Yoshawa were joined by rebels, equally made up of the downtrodden populace and Time Officers, whose uniforms were disguised by tattered rags and ghillie suits. At first they were joined by five, then a dozen, then thirty. By the time the echoes of the battle cry died out, the rebels stood as a group of over sixty strong, facing the eight armed guards, who grew increasingly more nervous by the second.

The "head guard", or the guy that had been their mouthpiece anyway, issued a toothless threat. "Leave the prisoner and disperse now!" The wall of angry rebels didn't respond or move an inch, they simply stared down the small assemblage of guards that they vastly outnumbered. "Call in backup!" the nervous guardsman screamed.

Before his subordinate could lift his com device, a bullet fired from the other side ripped through the device and the hand holding it, leaving the guard wounded and screaming in agony.

A deafening wall of gunfire erupted from both sides.

Chapter 14

The underground rebels had launched a full-scale assault on Project Magenta, their determination to set things right propelling them forward. Alecia, Gabriel, and Frank led the charge, their hearts pounding with a mixture of hope and desperation.

Bullets and fists flew haphazardly, but the swarm of rebels made short work of 8 armed guards.

Without a moment's rest, bullets began slamming into the concrete facade of the building around Alecia's head, several rebels fell. A massive mob of the poor, hungry and greedy, looking for a $4,000,000 payday had gathered, attacking the rebels from behind, pressing them toward the compound. Alecia dropped her fading cattle-prod and drew her sidearm from its holster. She hated the idea of killing anyone, but in this instance, she knew that her people were outnumbered and there was little to no choice. Amid the melee she fired several shots into the crowd that was screaming for her blood and their money.

Officer Morgan released a barrage of cover fire from an automatic weapon he'd removed from a guard as he approached Alecia. She was now ducking inside of an alcove, avoiding enemy gunfire, just inside of the security gate. "More security and Time Officers are going to be here any second, we have to move!" Alecia nodded in implicit agreement, there was no going back. The mission needed to be completed or she would die trying. "Alpha squad, close the door!" In response to Morgan's command, the remaining rebels moved like a well oiled machine. The majority of rebels moved through the security gate in a fluid motion, while a group of about 15, what was left of the Alpha squad, made a human wall across the security gate, weapons raised. A group of 15 was meant to keep out what seemed like the entire city that pursued them. The wall of the desperate and destitute pressed forward. Gunfire erupted from both sides once again, which was a signal to the rest of the rebels to move double-time, into the cold and sterile hallways of Project Magenta, as quickly as the bravery of their doomed comrades would allow.

A platoon of about 20 armed guards marched down the sterile white halls, toward the security gate. As they rounded the corner, they were momentarily taken by surprise, not expecting to come face to face with the rebels, never expecting that they had actually breached security. The element of surprise was not wasted, with several rebels taking the opportunity to thin the guards ranks before they could pull back to the cover of the crossing hallway.

Morgan approached Alecia in a doorway. "The longer this takes, the harder it will be, there is no shortage of guards and officers compared to us. We have to keep moving forward or we'll never make it." "Good thing I brought this." Yoshawa's smiling face interjected, lowering an automatic weapon in his hand and hefting a stainless steel grenade from his vest. The jovial asian grinned as he pulled the pin, dropped the grenade and kicked it mid-air, sending it careening down the hall to land roughly in front of the hunkered down platoon of guards. A guard began a panicked scramble, but too late. It was a concussion grenade. The kind that don't use shrapnel or do a lot of explosive damage, but are meant to stun with light and sound. An intense blinding light of exploding phosphorus was accompanied by a deafening bang. The rebels had paused to cover their ears, for what little good it did. Most of the guards were laid out or scrambling in disorientation, exactly the effect that such a grenade was meant to cause. A light gray smoke wafted and filled the hallways from the location of the explosion. Ears still ringing, Morgan gave the order to press on, taking advantage of the momentary disorientation of their enemies.

Led by Morgan, closely followed by Alecia and Yoshawa, the rebels moved down the hall, turning right, away from the smoke and bedraggled guards. A squad of rebels protected their rear as voices and gunshots began to resume from the stunned guards. The compound's security forces were being joined by additional officers, rushing in to help their colleagues from a doorway far down the hall. By the sounds starting to emanate from their former location, Alecia surmised that the wall of poor and downtrodden that had been fighting the rebels at the gate, were now inside the compound. With the Time Force locker room coming into view the trio leading pushed toward the goal, breaking into a sprint just in time for a side door to open, allowing the butt of an automatic rifle to smash hard into Alecia's face.

Alecia's mind scrambled to reorient itself after momentarily losing consciousness. She looked up at her attacker to see a large, muscular female Time Force officer with Orange shoulder pads standing over her menacingly, holding the rifle that she had just used to make Alecia lose that vital moment of consciousness. This woman had apparently been joined by several armed Time Officers, who were keeping Morgan and the other rebels engaged in battle. Alecia scrambled, still disoriented and feeling around for a weapon. Her startled gaze remained on the woman who was now leveling the rifle on her. The lightning quick hands of Yoshawa gave her weapon a quick jerk, causing it to fire into the ceiling. Moving like a striking snake, his quick bursts and short, sharp strikes left the woman disoriented and disarmed. Yoshawa stepped back and delivered a jump-kick to the woman's ribs, sending her reeling backward into the darkened room that she had emerged from earlier.

Alecia had taken advantage enough of her rescue that her scrambling hands had managed to find her sidearm. As Yoshawa grinned and reached out a hand to help her up, Alecia drew her gun and fired, taking out the Time Officer that had been approaching from Yoshawa's rear. "Well I guess I can't say you owe me," Yoshawa beamed as he helped Alecia to her feet. Morgan sent another Time Officer to dreamland with an elbow to the face, followed by a left hook. He looked at Alecia and spoke one word, "Move!". As she scrambled toward the Locker Room, she looked back to see the muscular woman, angrier than ever, emerge from the shadows and lock her arms around Yoshawa's chest, squeezing hard. Yoshawa, wide eyed, knew that Alecia's concern for him would not serve the mission. "Go!" Yoshawa yelled, before planting the back of his head into the angry woman's face, breaking her nose and eliciting an angry howl. Alecia ran through the locker room, past several surprised Time Officers that were in the middle of suiting up. Rebels, security guards and Time Officers spilled into the locker room in a wave following behind her.

The hallways of the compound had been overtaken by the desperate citizens of Los Angeles tent city. The mob had whipped into an unreasoning fervor. Time Officers and rebels alike were attacked by those who had been so oppressed that they no longer cared who they fought. Many no longer even cared about the reward promised for the fugitive. They had penetrated the impenetrable, the stronghold of a system that had taken any hope they had for life. While some still searched for a payday, others lashed out at guards, walls, windows, it was a riot. Security Officers struggled pointlessly, voices choked in their throats as they were beaten down and trampled before they could fire a warning shot.

Morgan followed as Alecia crossed the threshold between the locker room and the time lab. Several scientists and Time Officers lounged about in the smoky room, dazed and only semi-aware of the proceedings thanks to whichever drug of choice they were indulging in. As the pair eyed the control panel, angry voices of combatants echoing from the room behind them, their ears heard the ominous sound of a single pair of heavy boots clanging slowly across the metal grated floor from the other side of the room.

As the pair's eyes apprehensively found the sound, the confident figure and cocky expression of Kevin Kilroy approached, arms open, hands raised up in a godlike gesture of superiority. "You thought you could invade the most secure facility in the world? DO you even have any idea how many..." BLAM! Kilroy's gloating was cut-off by a gunshot, the bullet ripping through his shoulder and laying him flat on the floor, screaming in agony. Alecia returned her sidearm to her holster. "I owed you that one, asshole!"

An urgent hand fell on Alecia's shoulder, she turned to see Morgan gesturing to the Time Well controls. "Go!"

Morgan turned to face the approaching horde of combatants beginning to enter the time lab as Alecia crossed the platform and hit the necessary button to bring the Time Well online. Gunshots were already ricocheting off the shiny metal walls. She knew she had no time to see if this version of the timeline had the technology to shift the energy that allowed more pinpointed travel. As the glowing pink energy began to ripple across the open pit, Alecia scrambled up the metal grated support wall that held multiple video screens of time travel data. She had to make sure that she traveled back far enough to prevent this world from ever happening. For a brief moment Alecia looked around, above the rebels and guards fighting across the lab. She saw Yoshawa, free of his earlier rival, doing his best to hold back the wall of angry citizens that was now taking over the entire base and crushing everyone in their path. She looked and saw the angry Kilroy crawling toward the Time Well platform, teeth clenched, silently glaring his hatred at Alecia, his good hand holding the bleeding wound on his shoulder.

Alecia tipped forward, releasing the metal grating and tumbling forward through space. She held the icy glare of Kilroy, extended an arm, and displayed her middle finger toward this world's Time Director as she fell into the rippling pink energy.

Chapter 15

Alecia opened her eyes to find herself in her childhood bedroom. The familiar posters of her favorite bands adorned the walls, and the soft glow of the afternoon sun filtered through the curtains. It was a time before the painful memories of her mother's death, a time when life felt innocent and full of possibilities. It took a few minutes of staring at the ceiling and just breathing for Alecia to accept the reality of her situation, and that the last several days of her life hadn't been a horrible nightmare. She sort of wished it had been.

The fact was that her war-torn, tortured adult brain had a day to live in her five-year old body. She climbed out of bed clad in a soft, warm full body onesie with pink flower prints all over it, her small feet padding across the well-worn carpet. A wave of nostalgia washed over her as she wandered through the house, taking in every detail. The scent of freshly baked cookies wafted from the kitchen, drawing her in like a moth to a flame.

There, in the cozy kitchen, stood her mother, humming a tune while pulling a tray of cookies from the oven. Alecia watched her mother's face light up as she turned to see her daughter. It was a moment she thought she'd never experience again. Alecia was frozen, stunned with open mouthed silence. She knew when she'd woken up, but her brain hadn't put together that this was more than a full year before her mother had died.

"Mom," Alecia finally managed to whisper, her voice choked with emotion, before running forward and burying her young face in a deep, full bodied hug with her mother. Her mother's eyes sparkled with warmth as she embraced Alecia, the two of them holding onto each other as if they could stop time itself. "I love you so much mom." Alecia said, doing her best to sound upbeat and choke down the emotional tears of her adult self, before her mother noticed. "I love you too, dear," her mother responded with a surprised chuckle.

Tears welled up in Alecia's eyes as her mind battled with itself about what to do, what to say to her mother. Should she try to stop her mother's death? Alecia's conscience was already telling her that any attempt to do so would just take this whole time travel mess and make it more complicated and convoluted. "Can we have a day together, just you and me?" Alecia asked, hoping that at some point her intelligence and courage would combine to answer the doubts in her mind. "Aren't you the sweetheart this morning?" her mother replied. "Well, you're dad's gone to some estate auction today looking for old car parts, and I'm not working, so I don't see why not."

Alecia's mother June wasn't a physically imposing woman, but Alecia knew that her 5 '3" frame could be surprisingly intimidating when she meant business. June's temper was something anyone rarely saw though, reserved for only the most deserving occasions. "You go grab the eggs from the fridge and I'll make breakfast." She instructed Alecia with a smile. Alecia was more than happy to comply. She looked at the long blonde hair, blue eyes and wide-smile that she had been missing for so long, she thought she'd nearly forgotten it. Alecia watched her mother mix the pancake batter, chatting about things like life and school as they sizzled on the griddle and Alecia helped to clean up the flour spilled on the countertop. Alecia's young face grinned at the stack of plate-sized pancakes placed in front of her, more than she knew she ever had a hope of eating, but was willing to try. The two Hernandez girls enjoyed their pancakes and planned how they would spend their day together, June sipping her coffee and Alecia looking for new ways to attack her pancakes that would make more of them fit in her belly. "We could go for a bike-ride?" June suggested. "Oh, to Sand Harbor?" June knew that the local state park was one of her young daughter's favorite places. "Of course." she replied with a smile. "Can we rent a paddle board?". June chuckled at Alecia's excitement. "Sure, if you want to go paddle boarding, we can do that."

Alecia took a few minutes to get used to the fact that she was in a smaller body, riding a smaller bike than she'd experienced in years. Everything seemed more real than the daily adult life that she was used to. Air seemed fresher, colors seemed brighter, but none of that helped her adjust to the much lower center of gravity than she was used to. Her progress was a little wobbly at first, but after a few minutes, she was zipping past her mother and barrelling toward adventure. Soon, they were riding bikes through the neighbourhood, laughing and reminiscing about previous adventures at the state park. Alecia mentioned a story of their last visit when they came across a massive desert tortoise sunning itself on a sandy patch of beach sand, probably looking for a place to lay eggs or slowly make its way to the sandy shore for a drink and to dip its toes in the cool water. Tortoises didn't swim in the water like the local sea turtles did, a fact that young Alecia was very proud of knowing.

The pair were soon leaving civilization, biking down sidewalkless roads with gravel shoulders and lined with tall trees. Soon they turned off of the road entirely, following a familiar and well-worn wilderness trail. Alecia breathed in the scents of the cedar and white fir trees that stood tall all around them, providing protective shade from the hot sun to the people and forest floor below. After about 20 minutes of biking the pair emerged onto a sandy shoreline, too cumbersome to the bike tires for riding. They dismounted and walked toward a handful of beach goers, enjoying the sun and sand next to the paddle-board rental stand.

After locking their bikes to the nearby rack, June and Alecia were served by a bright-eyed teenage girl whose thick glasses reflected the sunlight beating down. Alecia had the brief thought that this girl was likely working at the park for the summer to save up some money. She smiled at both of them pleasantly as she stepped through the doorless archway, to pass the boards and paddles that they had rented to them.

A few minutes later, after Alecia had to adjust to this smaller body and board by tipping into the water and laughing several times, the pair were gliding along the mirror-like surface of Lake Tahoe. The water was calm and the mother and daughter took in the wonder of the wilderness, pointing out to each other when they spotted bald eagles and beavers, and waving to nearby boats as they coasted lazily along the lake's surface.

As much as the pair loved the experience of sliding atop the lake like a toboggan skidding across ice, their arms eventually grew tired from paddling, so they decided to head back to shore. Alecia picked out a nice warm sandy patch near the bike racks, and June produced a checked table cloth from her backpack. The pair enjoyed the picnic lunch that they'd prepared together before leaving the house. As Alecia sucked back on a grape Kool-Aid jammer, her mind wandered, thinking about all the experiences of the day that she hadn't realized that she'd been missing in her adult life, and the hole that had been left in it by the loss of her parents. In short order, a mix of timelines and experiences, along with her memories of Dale and his illness had joined that already crowded concerns in her tiny head. Her young face wasn't meant for hiding such heavy thoughts. "What's the matter honey?" her mother's voice broke Alecia out of her trance-like state. "Do you not like your sandwich?" "No, this sandwich is awesome." Alecia was emphatic, she loved her mom's leftover eggplant parm sandwiches. "I was just thinking..." "About what, honey?" June quizzed. Alecia thought for a moment. She was torn. She wanted to explain so much to her mother, but she knew that any major information or drastic changes might change the future for the worse, in unpredictable ways. One side of her mind was screaming "Tell her everything, that you love her and that you don't want her to die!", while another side of her brain was lecturing, "You've screwed up things enough already, don't say anything or you'll just make it worse." Alecia decided to aim for somewhere in the middle. "Do you ever think about what it will be like when we're gone?" "You mean like, what would this place be like if there were no people?" June responded. "Well there'd probably be more eagles and otters. The woods would be thicker...and they'd be filled with grizzly bears!" With that, June made a large claw-like gesture with her hands, growling like a fake bear and ticking Alecia with her imaginary claws, eliciting breathless pleas to stop. The distraction convinced Alecia that now was not the right time to bring up thoughts of the future. The mother and daughter, satiated from a great meal, laid back on the picnic blanket and looked at the clouds that soared over the tallest of the Sugar Pine trees, pointing out the ones that were shaped like a rabbit, a volkswagen and other misplaced objects of the sky. Alecia rolled over and hugged her mom again. "I love you, mom." "I love you too, baby."

After the pair struggled to pack the picnic stuff in the backpack, it never fit back in the same way, it was another twenty minute bike ride through the forest and back to their suburban neighborhood. The mother and daughter placed their bikes back on the rack that was mounted on the back wall of her father's workshop, and Alecia helped June with some quick housecleaning that she'd been putting off all week.

After the living room floor had been vacuumed, June pulled the coffee table and small furniture items into the corners of the room, making a nice big open space of the living room's hardwood floor. Without a word, June opened an old cabinet that sat against the wall and pulled out a record player, setting it on the aforementioned coffee table where it stood in its temporary corner home. She returned to the cabinet to retrieve a milk crate full of old records. Though relatively new pressings, most of them were remastered recordings that ranged from current hits, back to over 100 years of pop music.

They put on records of old music and danced in the living room, their laughter mingling with the music, until Brian Hernandez returned from his auction excursion. He entered through the workshop door into the living room to see his two girls dancing, smiling and giddily jumping about to greet him. He responded in his usual laughter, hugging his girls and joining in with some of the silliest dance moves that he could think of. Afterward, Brian quickly ran out to the garage and back in, to retrieve and present a gift to Alecia that he'd bought at the auction. A vintage pair of safety goggles that she could use when working together on their vehicle projects. She loved the old brass lens frames and held the goggles that her adult mind fondly remembered as if they were a cherished teddy bear.

The day's activities had taken a toll on everyone and the trio were soon cuddled together on the couch. Alecia enjoyed the feeling of being pressed snugly between her mother and father, looking up to see the love that was evident when the pair looked into each other's eyes. Happy and exhausted, Alecia fell into a deep afternoon nap.

Chapter 16

As Alecia tumbled out of the Time Well, the world around her seemed to shift back to the familiar and mundane. She glanced down at herself and found that she was once again clad in her mechanic's coveralls, a stark contrast to the bewildering adventures she had experienced thus far, but also a mild relief.

Muffled voices could be heard above as she cautiously climbed the rungs of the seemingly endless ladder. She did however, make it to the top of that ladder. Before she could fully comprehend her surroundings, a squad of heavily armed officers surrounded her, their weapons trained on her as if she were a dangerous criminal. "Come out with your hands up!" A Security Officer barked. Alecia complied nervously, at once filled with hope at how similar this timeline was to her original one, but tempered with the trepidation of having to face the consequences of unapproved time travel. They didn't give her a chance to speak, swiftly apprehending her and escorting her through a maze of sterile, metallic hallways.

Alecia was led into the small, dimly lit debrief room where the director of the Time Force awaited her. It was once again the older, sagging jowled man who had been the Time Director after her first jump. The stern expression on his face conveyed the gravity of the situation. She had been here before, recounting her unbelievable journey through time. The weight of her experience, the pain of the rebels, the pursuit of a crazed Kevin Kilroy, they all weighed on her, but had now, never actually happened. What seemed like hours to everyone else in the room had been days without end to Alecia. The weight of a half-dozen changed and erased timelines pressed down on a human mind that was not designed for such experiences. "Well," the Time Director glared, "What reason could you possibly have to throw away your freedom for the experience of Time Travel?" With a heavy sigh Alecia released a series of heavy sobs that she hadn't known she'd been holding. After a few minutes she was able to catch her breath and compose herself under the strict watch of the Time Director and several armed guards. Alecia looked up to the Time Director and in a pouring of emotion, she began to explain everything, the whole story, from the beginning.

The director listened intently, his gaze unwavering as Alecia laid out the intricate web of events that had transpired in her multiple time jumps. To his credit, the Time Director listened silently without interrupting the convoluted tale, filled with paradoxes and alternate realities, as Alecia spoke with unwavering conviction.

When she had finished, the director leaned back in his chair, steepling his fingers in thought. "IF this is in any way true," The Time Director responded finally, "This is a complex situation, with some very serious consequences, Mechanic Yoshawa. I clearly don't need to remind you of the consequences and unexpected side-effects of unsupervised changes to the timeline."

Alecia nodded solemnly, fully aware of the gravity of her actions. "I understand, sir. But I had to try to save him."

At that moment, the door to the room swung open, and to Alecia's surprise, her husband, Dale, was ushered in by another armed guard. Her heart soared at the sight of him, new memories of this timeline, where Dale didn't develop cancer, caught up with her ever straining mind. The rush of new memories added to that of all of the other timelines made her brain feel as if it would explode, she also felt a simultaneous joy. Tears filled her eyes. "Dale, oh my god, you're alive!" Alecia's frayed mental state quickly slipped from one of gratitude to one weighed down by the reality that she was about to face some serious consequences. "I'm so sorry." Alecia pleaded toward Dale.

Dale's expression was a mix of confusion and concern as he took the seat next to her, leaning over to embrace her. "Ali, what's going on? Why did you break into the Time Lab?"

"Well," interjected the Time Director, "We brought your husband here because he is a legitimate Time Officer and your story does affect him as well." Alecia hurriedly recounted a condensed version of her adventures to Dale, explaining the desperate measures she had taken to save him from a terminal illness. She watched his face closely, searching for any sign that he remembered their shared history, but there was none. It was as if the timeline had reset, erasing their past.

"I don't know if your wife is crazy, or if you're an accessory to some sort of time travel crime," The director interrupted their conversation, his voice filled with authority. "But I must caution you both that any changes made to the timeline were made illegally and, if possible, may need to be reversed. Before any decisions are made, you will both have to undergo a thorough debriefing and psych eval. There will be a hearing with the USDNA congress to determine the course of action. Depending on the result of that hearing, you may need to stand trial."

Alecia and Dale exchanged worried glances, well aware of the uncertain future that awaited them. Their moment of relief at being reunited was short-lived, overshadowed by the looming consequences of Alecia's desperate actions.

"You'll both need to be held in confinement, until I can confer with my colleagues and the Time Force legal department." Shocked, Alecia tried to reason with the head of the Time Force, "What? No! Put me in jail, but Dale didn't do anything." "So you say, MRS. Yoshawa, but from where I sit, you both need to be held on suspicion of illegal timeline tampering, until a proper LEGAL course of action can be taken."

With that, the Time Director stood, signaling the armed guards in the room to lift both Dale and Alecia from their chairs and cuff their hands behind their backs, ignoring the couple's continued pleas for freedom. Soon, they were escorted out of the room and into a waiting military transport vehicle. Alecia's hands were cuffed, and her mood was angry. She had nearly died, multiple times over, she had fought and fixed and brought her own husband back to life, and now, for all of her efforts, was likely to spend the rest of her days in a cell. Her face held a venomous glare, directed at everyone and everything around her.

Once secured together in the back of the armored prisoner transport vehicle, Dale leaned a comforting head on Alecia's shoulder. "I love you. I'm so sorry for what happened, and I believe you. I know you're not crazy." Alecia felt a slight relaxation at her husband's words, this man who always knew what to say had always been her perfect match, her soul mate. Her only response was to turn her face to his and kiss him while trying not to tear up again. "If any woman could bring me back from the dead to be with her, it would be you." Dale chuckled. "Yeah, and now we can spend the rest of our lives together, as prisoners." Alecia said with a sarcastic chuckle, a few tears managing to roll down her cheeks in spite of her efforts to suppress them. "They'd give us conjugal visits, right?" Dale asked, eliciting bitter sarcastic chuckles from both.

Eventually, the driver of the transport vehicle arrived. Without any acknowledgement of his prisoners, the armored officer started the vehicle's engine. Soon the shackled passengers felt the familiar feeling of liftoff, and the prisoner cargo vehicle rose into the air, high above Los Angeles, leaving the pair to silently contemplate their impending fate.

As the minutes passed, Alecia began to notice something amiss. The journey seemed to stretch on for far too long. Carefully, Alecia climbed up to stand on one of the benches that lined the sides of the prisoner containment area. Dale watched with a puzzled expression as Alecia adjusted to maintain her balance, not accustomed to having to do such things with her hands behind her back. "What are you doing?" Dale asked. Alecia didn't respond, at least not right away. Instead, she strained on her tippy toes, to peer out of one of the narrow slotted windows that lined the sides of the vehicle, allowing sunlight in for the prisoners inside. The scenery outside the armored windows didn't match her expectations.

Alecia hopped down from her perch to sit back down next to Dale, whose face expressed his curiosity and awaited response to his question. "Something's not right." Alecia said apprehensively. "We've been in the air too long, and we are nowhere near any Time Force holding facilities." "Where else would they be taking us?" Dale puzzled.

Growing suspicious, Alecia struggled to her feet, her cuffs jingling ominously. She peered through a small wire mesh window that allowed prisoners to speak to the officers driving the vehicle, if they so choose. "Officer, I'd like to know where we are being taken for questioning?"

"The director chose me personally to take you to military prisoner holding until the civilian authorities can arrive to pick up," a familiar voice that Alecia couldn't yet place answered. "Bullshit, we're not even heading in the direction of the holding facility."

"You got me!" the familiar voice chuckled, dropping any pre-tense of authority. The driver turned to make eye contact with Alecia. With a wry grin, Kevin Kilroy admitted, "I may have, uh, borrowed this vehicle before the actual assigned driver could get to it. He got distracted with a bathroom break."

Chapter 17

As the military transport vehicle sped along, Kevin Kilroy's delighted chuckle filled the air. Alecia and Dale exchanged wide-eyed glances, completely surprised that Dale's investigative partner had absconded with their prisoner transport vehicle.

Kevin leaned forward and shared more details. "There's no way I'm taking you guys to holding. Officers Bullock and Crain are the ones officially assigned to your case, but we'll have made our grand escape long before those two idiots even realize anything is awry."

Alecia couldn't help but let out an excited laugh. "Thank god! We finally found a timeline where Kevin isn't a complete dick!"

The trio had a chuckle about that for a moment, before they began to feel the familiar sensation of the vehicle lowering itself vertically to land.

As the vehicle touched down, Alecia and Dale braced themselves for whatever awaited them. The moment Kevin unlocked their manacles, Alecia took a step forward and asked, "Where have you taken us, Kevin?"

Kevin smirked. "You'll see."

With a mixture of dread and anticipation, Alecia and Dale exited the vehicle, their eyes scanning their unfamiliar surroundings. It didn't take long for Alecia's horror to set in as she realized they were standing on the roof of the Project Magenta compound, directly above the time lab.

"Why are we back at Project Magenta, Kevin?" Alecia asked, suspicion creeping into her voice. "Oh well, I just figured the best way to lose them and make them think we were running was to do a big loop and then come right back here after they just sent everyone to go find us." "Why are we here?" Alecia repeated.

"Isn't it obvious yet, hon?" Kevin replied. He drew his handgun, a standard issue for Time Officers during investigations, and pointed it at Alecia. Her heart raced as she met his cold, calculating gaze.

"You're going to go inside and jump in the Time Well," Kevin declared, his voice dripping with malice. "Undo what you've done, stop messing up all my hard work."

Alecia clenched her fists, defiant. "You can't make me undo it, Kevin. I did this because I love Dale."

Kevin's expression darkened, his obsession with Alecia shining through. "Love, Yoshawa? You think this is love? This is destiny. Fate. I've been watching you for so long, and I know we're meant to be together. I'll do whatever it takes to make you see that." With that, Kevin's aim was shifted to Dale, who was standing closer to their fake rescuer, still struggling to release one of his manacles. In a split second, before Alecia could react, Kevin squeezed the trigger of his handgun. The deafening gunshot echoed across the rooftop, and time seemed to slow as Alecia watched in horror as the bullet struck Dale in the head.

Her husband's eyes widened in disbelief, blood staining his shirt as he crumpled to the ground, his life slipping away. Alecia screamed, her world shattering as the man she loved lay dying before her. "Do you know how many jumps I had to make, the effort and planning put in, just to get the depleted uranium pellets I'd been planting around him for years to cause his cancer? And then you had to get involved and fuck things up, I had to undo half my work just to keep from tipping my hand too early. This has been an incredible investment in time and effort on my part!" Kilroy ranted.

Kevin stood there, his gun once again pointed at Alecia, a twisted smile on his face. "Now, Mechanic Yoshawa, are you ready to do as you're told?"

All of the strange, inexplicable changes to the timeline that Alecia had blamed herself for somehow creating all made sense. Kilroy had been tampering with the timeline all along, probably before Alecia had ever made her first jump.

Tears streamed down Alecia's face as she looked down at the lifeless body of the man she had fought so hard to save. The weight of her choices and their consequences bore down on her, and she had no choice but to comply with Kilroy's demands, in the hopes that a chance at freedom would present itself, knowing that there was only one course of action that she could take in order to save Dale.

Chapter 18

The Time Lab's roof entrance seemed to loom over Alecia as Kevin stood behind her, his gun digging into her back. With her heart pounding and her mind racing, she had no choice but to comply with his crazed demands.

Kevin forced Alecia to descend into the lab, her trembling hands reaching for the Time Well's control panel. Her movements were mechanical, her actions driven by the gun pressed against her spine.

As she activated the Time Well, Kevin's manic laughter filled the room. He stood there, gloating wildly, the fire of obsession burning in his eyes. "You see, Alecia, you'll undo everything you've done, including all my hard work. You'll love me, and you'll be obedient."

Giddy and deranged, Kevin continued, "I'll never give up, even if I have to kill Dale a hundred different ways. I'll keep coming back, manipulating time until you're mine."

With a wicked grin, Kevin tossed his gun aside and leaped into the Time Well, disappearing into the swirling vortex. Alecia had no other choice but to grab the gun and follow him.

- - -

When Alecia woke up, she was back in her college dorm, senior year. Panic surged through her. Muscle memory made her check for the gun she'd grabbed, knowing that it would not be there in her hand, even if it felt like it was just there. Her mind did a quick estimation that if she and Kevin made the same jump at the same time with the same momentum, they COULD have traveled back to the same day. She leaped out of bed, hastily getting dressed. Ignoring the puzzled questions of her dorm mates, she rushed out without explaining herself fully, desperate to find Kevin.

Alecia sprinted back and forth haphazardly across the UC Berkeley campus, scanning the surroundings for any sign of her enemy. After 20 minutes she was leaning over, panting with exhaustion. Alecia knew that she had to mentally regroup and come up with a better strategy. Taking a deep calming breath, she looked up, to see Kevin standing behind a bench across the courtyard, staring right at her. As she spotted him, he raised a hand and began waving and grinning. Alecia bolted toward him with new energy, but Kevin managed to evade her. He slipped behind the corner of a faculty building and by the time she had rounded that corner, he had once again disappeared. She kept moving at a quick pace, searching for her quarry. Alecia was relentless in her pursuit, but soon felt like she was falling back into the ill-advised search pattern that she's started with.

Alecia once again stopped to breathe, fighting back tears of frustration. Exhausted,she heard Kevin's taunting voice from behind. "Hey Leeash, how's it goin'?" He was laughing, standing in front of the school's study hall. The fact that he wasn't running any more gave Alecia the impression that he'd made the mistake of deciding not to run any longer. With a scowl of rage, Alecia silently marched toward her prey. Kevin urged her to stop, "Come on now hon, you don't wanna do anything that's gonna make the timeline worse or jeopardize you getting a job with Project Magenta." Alecia's expression remained unchanged and her quick threatening pace toward Kevin did not waiver. "We could work together, maybe that's the best way to make a world that we both want."

Without responding, Alecia was now silently face to face with the obsessed tormentor who had manipulated her life for his own ends. With a sudden burst of anger, she kicked him through the plate glass window of the library, causing a loud shattering sound that disrupted the quiet of the study hall and drew the attention of students who had been deeply engrossed in study material.

Alecia walked through the shattered window frame and descended upon Kevin, determined to end this once and for all. She pummeled him with furious punches, shouting curses at him. "You fucking piece of shit! You're pathetic!" The fact that Kevin was laughing the whole time while blood from cuts and punches ran down his face did not help to calm Alecia's temper.

The library soon became a battlefield as Alecia and Kevin engaged in a vicious brawl. They fought across the library, colliding with computers, book trolleys, and terrified students and staff who had gathered to watch the chaotic spectacle.

Kevin continued to gloat, his words filled with arrogance and defiance. "Willpower is the only true cause worth following in life, Alecia. Willpower and desire are stronger than the idea of soul mates and romantic love. My willpower has done more to change and shape this world than love ever has." Alecia, undeterred, grabbed him by the collar and delivered a powerful punch to his nose, breaking it. Despite the pain and blood, Kevin laughed and spat at her. "What are you going to do Alecia?" Kevin asked defiantly, blood running down his face. "Huh? What can you do? The situation has become too unstable and unpredictable to kill me, especially in front of all of these witnesses."

Surrounded by campus security, Alecia saw tasers pointed at her. She punched Kevin once more, hard. She felt his body go limp below her and realized that she had knocked him unconscious. Alecia looked at the guards, screaming at her to cease and desist, perhaps a little hesitant to use their weapons when a young woman was the aggressor. Alecia screamed at the guards desperately as she lunged towards them, "Come on you fucking cowards!" Before she could finish her demand, one of the guards fired his taser, and Alecia grinned down at Kevin as she was shocked into unconsciousness.

Chapter 19

Alecia and Kevin tumbled out of the Time Well and onto the airbag. Their clothes had undergone subtle changes again, reflecting the alterations in the timeline. Alecia cursed under her breath "Fuck!" as she quickly scanned their surroundings. The gun she had grabbed earlier had vanished, erased from existence in this new reality.

No sooner had they landed than they resumed their violent struggle. It was a fight fueled by desperation, each of them trying to gain the upper hand. Alecia managed to scramble toward the ladder, and the two of them fought fiercely to be the first one back up to the top.

When they reached the surface, Kevin wasted no time, leaping back into the Time Well. Alecia, her determination unwavering, jumped in after him.

What followed was a relentless cycle of falling out of the Time Well, fighting, and scrambling back up to jump in again. With each fall, their clothes morphed slightly, sometimes more drastically, reflecting the ever-changing timelines they were thrust into. Any injuries or battle damage they incurred during their fights were reset with each jump, left behind in the past as they returned to the Time Well.

If a person was a fly on the wall, with a good vantage point, it would have appeared as if the scenery of the time lab morphed and melded into slightly different configurations each time the pair fell through the glimmering pink energy, their clothes morphing as quickly as the room around them.

With every leap, Alecia and Kevin found themselves in strange and altered versions of reality. They clashed in various environments, their battles becoming increasingly brutal and chaotic. Each time one of them lost consciousness, they were drawn back to the Time Well, where they would clash and race to the ladder once more.

It was an agonizing loop, a never-ending sequence of violence and uncertainty, where time itself seemed to warp and twist around them.

Finally, after countless cycles, they dropped back into a present that seemed both familiar and foreign. Alecia found herself in her original high-tech mechanics overall. Kevin's gun lay loose on the crash padding. The pair scrambled desperately toward the weapon. A well placed knee to Kilroy's face gave Alecia the edge needed to grab the gun first. She stood clutching the gun, keeping it pointed at her enemy with no sign of wavering.

Kevin attempted to talk his way out of the situation, his words dripping with manipulation and deceit. "Okay, okay you've got me. Listen, Alecia, going to jail won't help. I'll work with you, we can get Dale back." But Alecia had endured too much, seen too many realities unravel to trust the word of Kevin Kilroy. Her resolve remained silently unshaken. Without a word, she raised the gun and fired two shots. Kevin crumpled to the ground, blood staining his clothes.

Exhausted and haggard, Alecia turned away from the fallen man and began the arduous climb up the ladder, leaving behind the chaos of time and violence, and seeking the solace of the present.

Chapter 20

As Alecia continued her climb up the ladder, she felt a sudden, violent jerk that threatened to pull her back into the abyss below. It was Kevin, bloodied and maniacal. "I'll never stop Alecia, that's how much I love you!" Refusing to let go of their twisted cycle of jumping, fighting, and chasing each other through time was not a part of Alecia's long-term plan, not that she really had one at this point. Kevin's maniac grin taunted her. "Maybe this endless battle is our destiny?" Alecia knew that Kevin would never allow her to find peace as long as he couldn't have her, and Dale would never be safe. At the moment it was taking all of the energy that her limbs had left just to slow his progress, attempting to climb up onto her body to grab a hold of her.

"Look at all of the changes that my will has wrought upon society. Who's to say that I'm not a god?" Kevin pleaded, refusing to relinquish his grip on her ankle, struggling his way up to overtake her. Alecia knew he had affected great amounts of change during their endless loops, but she also understood that sometimes, desire alone wasn't enough.

With a sinister determination, Alecia spoke calmly to Kevin, her voice carrying an air of subtle menace. "You may have changed the world a lot, Kevin, but you should never mess with someone who knows the inner workings of the Time Well." She reached into her coveralls and pulled out an electric ratchet, removing several bolts from a metal wall panel halfway up the ladder. The panel clanged as it fell to the ground, revealing long, thick coolant hoses hidden behind it.

Alecia deftly grabbed one of the hoses, coiled it to gain some slack, and wrapped it around Kevin's neck before he could react. With a swift, forceful kick, she sent him tumbling off the ladder. Kevin's scream filled the pit as he was choked by the hose, his body convulsing and swinging like a grotesque marionette. He gasped for air, struggling to break free, but the noxious coolant leaking from the ruptured hose only added to his torment.

Alecia watched with a wearied expression as Kevin's struggles grew weaker, his face turning an alarming shade of blue. After a few seconds, she calmly ripped the hose from the wall, causing a gush of coolant to splash in all directions and Kevin's heavy, limp body to crash back down to the floor. Exhausted and emotionally drained, she continued her ascent up the ladder, finally reaching the top.

When she emerged from the Time Well pit, she found herself surrounded by stunned witnesses, including Dr. Agu, the Time Director, Benny Hurley and a contingent of security guards and Time Officers. She let out a deep breath and muttered, "I think he might still be alive down there."

The Time Director stepped forward, his expression a mix of concern and relief. "Yoshawa, we need you to tell us what the hell just happened."

Alecia began to recount her story once more, her voice tinged with exhaustion and frustration. However, Dr. Agu interrupted her gently, "Sir, Mechanic Yoshawa, we've retrieved everything we need from the recording microphones inside the Time Well. We've got everything Kilroy confessed to down there."

Several burly officers descended into the pit to retrieve Kevin, whose unconscious body was quickly strapped to a med gurney with a beeping vital screen attached. "When he wakes up, he's going to realize that he'll never taste freedom outside of four walls again." The Time Director stated. Kevin's prone form was hauled away to a medical transport for emergency attention, then likely the same holding compound that the Yoshawa's had been destined for earlier, in a different timeline

As the chaos began to subside, Alecia couldn't help but feel a profound sense of relief. The nightmarish journey through time, the relentless battles, and Kevin's twisted obsession were finally over. With the support of her friends, her love for Dale, and the knowledge that she had set things right, Alecia could now look toward the future with hope and the promise of a better tomorrow.

Chapter 21 - Epilogue

Alecia took a breath, setting down her notes, she looked up at the large auditorium at UC Berkeley that was filled to capacity with eager time travel mechanical engineering students. They were all hanging on the edge of their seats in rapt silence, waiting to hear what this extraordinary woman would say next. She stood at the lectern, her confidence and authority as evident as the anticipation of her audience.

"What had started as a personal journey exploring morality became an important lesson for not only Project Magenta, but the whole world. Thankfully, my ill-advised violation of protocol undid most of the damage done by Kilroy's manipulations. In some cases, we corrected things, like reinstating the panel of nine Time Directors. In other cases, I was lucky enough to have undone the damage that caused Dale's illness." With that, Alecia gestured toward Dale, who had been leaning against the wall by the entrance, watching Alecia give her lecture. Benny Hurley stood next to Dale, beaming with pride at his protege'. The attention of the entire auditorium shifted to that spot on the wall intently. Dale, smiling and a little embarrassed by the sudden attention, gave a small wave, which elicited a round of applause from the students and faculty in the room.

"What we need to remember most of all, is that time travel is the most important technology developed by man since the printing press, but in this case we can undo what was printed and reshape it so that life is better for everyone on Earth. The lesson to take from my story is not that it's okay to break the rules and reshape the past, but that we must be ever vigilant to guard against abuses and uphold the firm conviction to never let any one person use it for personal gain. To do so would mean disaster and suffering for everyone else. If we work together we can all ensure a better life and a better future for everyone. And that is the end of my lecture, thank you all for being here."

With Alecia's final words, the auditorium shifted from rapt silence to thunderous applause and cheering. Alecia smiled and waved, saying thank you to the crowd. Dale and Benny quickly walked to the side of the stage where Alecia had given her talk. Dale gave his own wave and then joined her in walking through the dark curtains that separated the speaker's area from the "back stage".

"Wow, they really loved that." Dale spoke excitedly. Blushing with pride, Alecia smiled, "It sure seems like they did!" "Hell of a job kid, inspiring." Benny praised, failing to hold back a couple of proud tears.

As Alecia turned to gather her things, a jacket and laptop bag that had been left on a chair behind the curtain, she felt a thin liquid running down her face. When she went to wipe it, a stark red smear spread across the back of her hand, leaving a bright red streak across her cheek.

She had a moment to turn and look at Dale and share a brief wide-eyed expression of surprise, before her eyes rolled back in her head and she flopped hard into the floor.

"Help! Call 911." Dale screamed as he knelt to hold Alecia's limp, bleeding, unconscious form.

- -

Soon, Dale was standing in a hospital, looking at the still, unmoving body of the woman he loved, connected to machines that beeped and displayed various metrics of life. She would almost look like she was peacefully sleeping, if the entire scenario hadn't been involuntary.

Dr. Grant looked at Dale with a mix of empathy and concern as she spoke. "At this point, all we know is that there was a brain aneurysm that burst and caused a hemorrhage, which put Alecia into a coma. It's too soon to say if we can perform a surgery to fix some of the damage, but even if we can, there's no guarantee that she will heal enough to regain consciousness."

"How did this happen?" Dale responded, fighting back tears and a well of emotions inside him that was waiting to burst out. "We don't know," the doctor answered disappointedly. "She's been exposed to more chronal radiation than anyone who's ever been studied. Could that have caused or contributed to the brain aneurysm? At this point we just can't say for sure, there's not enough data and no one else with her level of concentrated exposure."

"I...understand." Dale replied dejectedly, hanging his head. "Thank you doctor."

- -

That night, Dale scanned in through the security gate at Project Magenta, strode to the locker room and dressed in his time jump suit. Just as he was finished, he was greeted by Gail Agu, typically working much later than her shift demanded.

Gail was somewhat startled. "Officer Yoshawa, what are you doing here? I didn't see you on the schedule." Dale gave a stern reply, "You know why I'm here Gail."

Only moments later Dale was standing on the Time Well platform. Gail's fingers gingerly running over the control screens to ensure proper settings. The silent flashing lights warning of an unscheduled time jump were flashing all around, but security would never make it in time.

Dale stared into the rippling pink energy that crept across the cavernous mouth of the Time Well and dropped in.

About the Author

Meet Mike Gagnon, a Canadian author and illustrator bursting with creativity across various genres and mediums. From his early days delving into comic books and graphic novels, to captivating mature audiences with his written works like "Skidsville" and "A Western Gentleman," Gagnon's storytelling explores an eclectic range of genres.

His distinctive style and narrative skill have landed him collaborations with big names like Dark Horse Comics and Marvel Comics, as well as producing notable pieces like "The Island of Dr. Morose" and "Classics Illustrated: Royal Canadian Mounted Police."

But Gagnon doesn't stop there. He explores fiction, non-fiction, and screenplay writing, diving into themes ranging from science fiction to horror and mystery. With each project, he pushes the storytelling envelope, leaving an unforgettable mark on literature and illustration.

For more of Mike's captivating creations, check out www.mikegagnon.ca.

IP INFO

What does the notice above mean?:

So, you've stumbled upon "Project Magenta" and you're itching to know what this whole Creative Commons license jazz is about?

Alright, let's start with the basics. "Project Magenta" is a story created by Mike Gagnon. He's poured his heart and soul into this story and now he's sharing it with the world. But here's the cool part: he's not just throwing it out there and hoping for the best. Nope, he's chosen to register it as a Creative Commons story.

Now, what exactly is this Creative Commons thing? Think of it like a toolkit for creators. It gives them a way to share their work with the world while still maintaining some control over how it's used. It's like saying, "Hey, feel free to use my stuff, but here are a few ground rules."

So, "Project Magenta" falls under the Attribution-ShareAlike 4.0 International license. Fancy name, right? But don't worry, it's not as complicated as it sounds. Let's break it down:

Attribution: This is all about giving credit where credit's due. If you decide to use anything from "Project Magenta"—whether it's the characters, the storyline, or even just the vibe—you've gotta tip your hat to Mike Gagnon. It's like saying, "Thanks for the inspiration, Mike!". So you have to acknowledge him with a credit in your project.

ShareAlike: Now, let's say you're feeling inspired by "Project Magenta" and you decide to create your own spin-off story or sequel. Awesome! But here's the deal: anyone who enjoys your creation has to know where it came from, and they've gotta play by the same rules you did. That means they've gotta use the same Creative Commons license. It's like keeping the creative party going and ensuring that everyone's on the same page.

Money: Now, here's where it gets interesting. You might be thinking, "Can I actually make money off my creations based on 'Project Magenta'?" The short answer is yes! You're free to sell your stories, adaptations, or anything else you come up with. But—and this is a big but—you've still gotta follow the rules of the license. That means giving credit where it's due and sticking to the same Creative Commons license. It's all about sharing and keeping the creative juices flowing while still respecting the original creator.

Copyright: Ah, but what about copyright, you ask? Good question! Even though "Project Magenta" is under a Creative Commons license, it's still copyright protected. That means Mike Gagnon owns the rights to his work, and you can't just go around reprinting it without his permission. So, while you're free to use his characters and stories in your own creations, just make sure you're not plagiarizing or reprinting the exact same story that has already been published.

Verification: But hey, don't just take my word for it! You can verify all this info by heading over to the Creative Commons website at www.creativecommons.org. There, you'll find all the nitty-gritty details about the Attribution-ShareAlike 4.0 International license.

Creative Help: Oh, and one more thing. If you're thinking about creating your own stories featuring the characters from "Project Magenta" and you need a writer or artist, guess what? You can hire Mike Gagnon himself! Yup, that's right. He might be available to work or consult on your project, so don't hesitate to reach out to him at www.mikegagnon.ca.

Conclusion: So, there you have it—everything you need to know about the Creative Commons license for "Project Magenta." It's all about sharing, giving credit, and keeping the creative juices flowing. So go ahead, dive into the world of "Project Magenta," and let your imagination run wild!

Don't miss out!

Visit the website below and you can sign up to receive emails whenever Mike Gagnon publishes a new book. There's no charge and no obligation.

https://books2read.com/r/B-A-RBQB-GNKZC

BOOKS 2 READ

Connecting independent readers to independent writers.

Also by Mike Gagnon

Skidsville
The Island of Dr. Morose
The Illusion of Freedom
A Letter to the Middle East
A Western Gentleman
Project Magenta

Watch for more at www.mikegagnon.ca.

About the Author

Mike Gagnon is an author living in the Niagara Region of Canada.

He has been a professional writer and comic creator since 2000. He has written, illustrated and edited hundreds of books, articles and graphic novels.

Mike has worked for publishers of all sizes, from Marvel Comics to many small press publishers.

He also enjoys teaching the crafts of writing and illustration to students of all ages with his workshops and seminars, as well as teaching at a prominent animation school in Toronto, Canada.

For more info visit: www.mikegagnon.ca

Read more at www.mikegagnon.ca.